OCTOBER SNOW

BOOK 1 OF THE FROST WITCH SAGA

BONNIE ELIZABETH

MY BIG FAT ORANGE CAT PUBLISHING

October Snow
My Big Fat Orange Cat
Urban Fantasy August 2020

Copyright 2020
Bonnie Elizabeth Koenig

Cover image Copyright © "Brazil", "donogl" | Deposit Photo

Cover Design Copyright © Bonnie Koenig

My Big Fat Orange Cat Publishing
MyBigFatOrangeCat.com

The snow had been silent, creeping up through the mid-October day and into the evening without even a slight breeze to indicate a storm was coming. Courtney McLaren watched the flakes from her front window as they fell softly, silently through the dark late-evening sky to find their place upon the ground where they joined with their fellow snowflakes to knit the light blanket of white which covered the neighborhood.

Inside the house, the heat clicked on, making Courtney jump. She turned, eyeing the worn, brown sofa that she'd gotten from her parents. Then she went back to watching the snow. She'd turned off the lights in the house to watch, to see how high the snow would pile. She felt... she didn't quite know what she felt. Odd.

Like she'd been waiting for this all her life.

Which was strange because while snow was exciting—Lexington, Kentucky didn't get a lot of snow—she couldn't say she loved snow. This snow made her five years old again, getting up on Christmas morning to find her new bicycle beside the tree, outshining her sister Payton's new Barbie roadster.

Courtney bit her lip, not sure why this snow drew her. She wanted to be out in it, dancing around. She wanted to go put on shorts and a t-shirt, ready to run out into the night and dance beneath the flakes. She was halfway across the room before it occurred to her what a ridiculous idea it was to go out in the cold and snow in such an outfit.

Instead, she paused to grab her jacket, which wasn't much more than a hoodie. She didn't need that much in a normal winter. Courtney put it on, frustrated when her arms got stuck in the sleeves, making her swear slightly under her breath, a habit she'd learned when she'd had roommates and parents and siblings who didn't like the fact that she could swear like a sailor.

Getting her arms through the hoodie, finally, she hurried through her kitchen, a room arranged such that she could have her table and chairs inside it, surrounded on two sides by espresso cabinetry. The stainless steel appliances gleamed even in the dim light she had on, which brightened the room. It also helped that she'd painted the room a very pale lavender gray which was picked up by her lavender kitchen towels.

Tonight it smelled like the pizza which she'd picked up on her way home from work. She had a passion for sausage, mushroom, and onion. The pizza place next to the medical clinic where she did billing made it perfectly with fresh mushrooms and sausage hotly spiced.

If her dad was going to interfere in her life enough to talk to her into buying a house instead of the condo she'd wanted, she'd insisted on the decorating scheme, something slightly wild. Something to annoy him, just a bit, like her swearing. She loved being a homeowner but hated being cut off from people the way she was in the house. Never mind that she could practically stretch out through her bathroom window to touch her neighbor's house. She didn't have someone on the other side of the wall snoring or singing or even annoyingly playing drums to keep her company.

And Courtney hated that.

A blast of cold hit her when she opened the backdoor and walked out under her covered patio. The trees along the back of the yard were bare of leaves this fall, their long limbs reaching towards her like the boney arms of a skeleton. The house behind her had on lights which sent shadows playing on her lawn, black snakes against the white blanket of snow.

Courtney shivered in the night air. She wished she had someone to share the moment with. Her ex-boyfriend Chase would have been good. Chase liked the outdoors. He did some sort of weird security work that never made sense to her. He lived almost dorm-style in a big old house not far from the University of Kentucky.

His housemates were weird. Courtney hadn't exactly disliked them at first, but they had all those cats. She wasn't a big fan of cats, who moved and jumped and tickled at the least opportune moments. She shuddered just thinking about it. Chase had almost always come to her house.

She'd suggested he move in last week, maybe leave the cat behind, and the next day, he'd decided things weren't working out. As if Trag—a stupid name for a stupid black cat—was more important than she was.

Courtney made a face and stepped out from beneath the safety of her covered patio. She raised up her arms and turned her face to the black sky, letting snow fall around her. She smiled as it touched her, feeling something deep inside her change. She felt stronger. As if the snow were making her stronger.

She hadn't felt that good since she'd broken up with Chase. She'd almost felt as if he'd taken something from her, but now she understood she'd just been waiting. For the snow to start falling so she could reimagine who she was against the blank white canvas the flurries provided.

Courtney looked down, feeling sad that she'd messed up the smooth blanket on her lawn with her footprints. Never mind. The snow was falling fast enough that those would fill in quickly.

She hurried back under the covered patio, the concrete cold beneath her feet which were slightly damp in her tennis shoes. She hadn't even thought to put on boots. She went inside, shaking out her wet hair and pulling off the sweatshirt that quickly dampened as the heat inside melted the flakes that had cuddled upon her shoulders.

The house creaked. The groan the settling foundation made sounded like someone calling out her name. "*Courtney.*"

At first, she wasn't bothered, but the sound came again, a hint of a groan. A bit of a whisper. A thing that was coming for her.

Suddenly the snow didn't feel like something she was waiting for at all. The blinds in the front room were open. The angle of the light from the neighbor's garage created a shadow with the tall oddly shaped bush that sat near her door. The shadow moved.

Courtney laughed at herself. Surely it was the wind that moved the shadow. Except the bush outside remained still. No sound came from her wind chime. Nothing. The shadow continued to dance.

The desire to laugh changed to a desire to scream, but her throat felt as if it had closed up upon itself and only the tiniest little whine came out of her mouth.

DREW

Drew watched Amber pace at the back window, looking out at the snow, her arms crossed in front of her chest. The cats were equally restless. He looked over at his big orange tabby, Mack, who was on one of the chairs in the breakfast nook looking out. The room smelled of years of garlic and onions and coffee. They'd probably have to strip the walls down to nothing before it smelled any different.

The house wasn't that old but plenty of people lived in it, plenty of activity through the years. Each of them had probably become inured to the smell of cat litter, which no doubt lingered beneath the other scents.

Everyone had their bond-mate cat, as they were called, in the house and each cat had his or her own litterbox. Of course, maybe being telepathically bound to a cat meant he didn't notice the smells from the litterboxes unless they needed cleaning? Drew was very aware that being a bond-mate to a cat had changed him.

The gas fireplace was on, though the lights were down. Chase was in the chair, looking irritated by everyone in the room. Tom and Tenny sat near the fireplace looking at their tablets. Chara, Tom's Siamese, a petite girl with a voice the size of Jupiter, laid practically up to the fireplace screen. While she was stretched out, every muscle in her body was on alert.

Like Amber.

Drew felt it. Felt Mack trying to discern what was going on with the unusual storm. Matt was out there, with his solid black cat, Wilbur, watching.

That's what they did in the house. They all watched. Matt, Anson, and Chase were the designated watchers, like point guards, sent out from the house to keep an eye on the portal which existed in the park around the corner.

Drew had lived his life in Lexington. He'd worked for numerous animal shelters and veterinarians. He was on an unofficial list of folks to call when a pet went missing and he spent more than his fair share of time searching out animals in various parks and neighborhoods throughout the city. Until a decade ago, when he'd become mind-bonded to Mack, he'd had no idea the park was anything but normal.

The portal wasn't visible to ordinary humans. Even now, Drew didn't see anything. Matt, who was out on watch that night, had once told him that he only saw something when the portal opened. Even then, it was more a sensation of a door opening to a new place. Sometimes, the shadows around him changed.

The portal only opened when a creature from another world came through. Based on Mack's description, Drew thought of the universes as bubbles floating in the air. Sometimes they floated close together and touched for a moment. At those times, something could slip through into the wrong world.

The person and their bond-mate cat watching would then push the creature back through the portal. Sometimes a host of creatures would come through, requiring more than one person to send them back. That had been Drew and Mack's job before Mack had reached his tenth birthday and officially retired.

Mack's age meant Drew was also retired. He could have taken Mack and gone to live somewhere else, but Drew liked it there. They called it the clowder house because a group of cats was a clowder. The house had been purchased by a group, which Drew only knew as *Base Command*, that administered the clowder houses around the world—or, if Mack were to be believed, worlds.

The cats were uniquely tuned to the portals. They had, in fact, been created to watch the portals. Before there were portals, the bubbles had come together in random spots, and creatures would come through, get lost in the wrong world, and die.

Drew wasn't clear on the details of the history of the portals. Nor did he fully understand their magic. He heard Mack sigh in his head, letting him know within their bond that Drew was disappointing him.

Still, history wasn't his thing. That was Riley's thing. Drew didn't dwell on it.

He was a worker. He liked animals, all animals, and was currently trying to figure out what he might want to do seeing he had no official duties at the house. Naturally, in addition to room and board, he got paid because he was bond-mate to Mack. Even retired, Mack was valuable to Base Command, but Drew wanted to do something. He just wasn't quite certain what it was.

Going back to working in shelters didn't quite appeal to him. He'd seen things that he'd never been able to imagine. One time, he'd encountered tiny little fairy-like things that buzzed around in a swarm like bees and had tickled him so hard he'd almost fallen over laughing as he had worked with

Mack and other bond-mates, human and feline, to send them back through the portal to their home.

The watcher cats knew how to read the portals and had known four of the fairy creatures were missing. Mack and Drew had spent hours searching the park for them. Mack had found one on the ground. Drew had carried it back. It, like the other three, was dead.

It had taken long enough that the watcher cat had had to reset the portal once the others were found, also dead, and send them through. Their deaths had affected Drew, made him sad. The creatures had made him laugh in ways he'd never laughed during his life before and then they were gone. It was as if their fairy-like lights had literally brought light into his heart and mind and just as suddenly they were taken from him.

"*Stop woolgathering,*" Mack said.

Drew would never have said woolgathering. Mack always sounded more educated than Drew was.

"*At least smarter,*" Mack agreed.

"The temperature has dropped over thirty degrees since this afternoon," Tom said. A few inches shorter than Drew, Tom was of medium height and weight. His dark hair was trimmed neatly, and he was, as always, clean-shaven, though Drew knew Tom often went and shaved after dinner to keep his face that smooth.

"*Riley hasn't yet come up with anything in the records about a creature that can change the weather like this,*" Mack said.

Drew sighed. They'd joked about frost witches earlier. Now, it might not be a joke. Frost witches were legends. Supposedly they came and ate the warm life spirit of the worlds, perhaps even the suns, and then left again. No world survived

"*They are,*" Mack said. "*Although all legends come from somewhere.*"

"I don't like it," Amber said. "It feels all wrong." Amber's tuxedo cat, Minnett, sat on the cat tree in the corner between the fireplace and the window. Her white front toes hung off the side as she worked to get her nose closer to the window so she could see better.

"It's snow," Chase said. "So it's that arctic blast or whatever the hell they're calling it this time. It happens every year."

"This wasn't forecast," Tom said.

Tenny didn't even bother to raise her head to look at him, as she continued to examine her tablet. Drew knew she was rolling her eyes at the comment. Chase had been difficult for the last week or so. Drew figured it was because he'd broken up with his girlfriend Courtney. It was hard having a partner that wasn't in the clowder house. There was so much that you couldn't say. Drew envied Julia and Cari who had each other.

Kayley's boyfriend was in the navy and he was deployed overseas. It meant she could tell him the good things about her life but didn't have to try and hide the times she was out searching around the city for creatures that didn't belong. In terms of not having to lie about her life, it worked well, but Drew knew Kayley missed the guy something awful.

Drew often ran out to the store at night to get a pint of Ben and Jerry's which the two of them would share while watching sappy old movies until Kayley felt better.

"So what? You want to go with frost witches?" Chase practically yelled. "I know that all legends are based in some fact, but that's ridiculous. Why would they even want to come here?"

"We were in the wrong place and they came through," Tom said quietly. That was how it normally worked with creatures.

"Except Matt hasn't seen anything come through."

Amber stopped her pacing, her face going white.

"I can't get Wilbur," Mack said. *"He's just gone silent."* All the cats could communicate with each other. It was how a cat on watch could contact others.

Tom pulled out his phone to call Matt. Drew leaned forward watching as the phone rang.

Tom shook his head when voicemail picked up.

"Something happened," Tenny said. She was already standing. Upstairs, Drew heard Julia and Cari rushing around to gather up clothing. They'd want to go after Matt. They were his backup, just as Tom and Tenny were Chase's. Fin and Kayley were Anson's. They all worked in teams. Amber was a healer. Riley was a researcher. And Drew was just an extra, kind of like he'd been all his life.

COURTNEY

Courtney hated the way the house was settling and creaking in the cold. She'd tried calling her dad, but the call didn't go through. She tried texting her best friend, Hannah, but her phone gave her a message it would send when it re-connected.

The creaks and groans seemed to be calling her name, "Courtney." It sounded like something in a creepy, old movie with bad special effects except that this was her life in her house.

Just yesterday it had been a happy enough place with a comfortable sofa, even if the sofa was older than Courtney herself. She'd been proud of the colors she'd painted the place, the lavender gray in the kitchen in an eggshell finish that meant the slight sheen reflected even dim light, brightening the otherwise dark room. She'd gone with a pale beige with lavender gray undertones for the rest of the house. She intended to paint her home office a bright lavender but hadn't gotten a color she liked well enough, yet.

"Don't go overboard on bright colors. Neutral tones are

better for resale," her dad told her, as if she were only going to live there for a year or so.

Back when she'd bought the place, maybe he'd been expecting her to marry Len, the guy she'd been dating then. He'd been an engineer and she'd been head over heels until she realized that Len was just as head over heels in love as she was, but with himself. When he'd gotten a job just outside Cincinnati, he'd expected Courtney to just pick up and move because it was good for him. As far as he was concerned she could find a job anywhere.

So her job wasn't exactly exciting in terms of a career. She was good at insurance billing and making sure the medical clinic got paid. She had a backbone at work, which was not something she apparently had in relationships with men.

And here she was, afraid in her own house and there were no men to call.

Courtney could hear her dad, "All houses creak and groan. Remember the time you thought there were monsters outside your window and it was a tree branch?"

She'd been seven years old. What did he expect? Yet, whenever she got scared being alone in the house, which happened more than she liked, her father would bring that up. When she'd first moved from her apartment building into the house, she'd come home and sleep at her folks or at Payton's once or twice a week because she'd been scared.

"You need to get over it," her dad said. "Stand on your own two feet. I can't make Payton send you home, but I want you to know that unless your house has burned to the ground or you're too ill to take care of yourself, you are not welcome to spend the night here anymore."

Courtney had gone home and cried, not even trying to argue with him.

She sniffed again.

If only Chase hadn't chosen his cat over her. How bad

was that? He wasn't even cheating on her with a human. He just preferred his cat. What kind of girl loses a guy to his cat? And it wasn't like she'd insisted he get rid of Trag, either. She'd suggested he move in with her and maybe Trag would stay at the big house where the others would take care of him.

But no. Chase had been quiet for a bit before leaving, saying he had to think about it. The next day he'd come by and basically shut her down, breaking up with her because he wasn't about to give up his cat. He said she clearly didn't know him at all if she could even suggest such a thing.

It wasn't even something he was willing to let her backtrack on. He was just out of her life. He'd even come prepared with a duffle bag to bring home the things he'd left there. Courtney had been crushed when he'd left the photo of the two of them at the fair on her dresser. It was still there, staring at her, reminding her of the failed relationship. The problem was, of course, that she hadn't a clue what to do with it. She didn't want to throw it out, not yet. She wasn't ready.

If Chase had been there, he'd have seen the shadows dancing on her floor where they had no right to be. She'd know she wasn't crazy.

He could tell her if the house groaned her name every time it settled or shifted. It happened every few minutes. Courtney had lived a lot of places and none of them had groaned and creaked like this house was doing that night. Even her little house was normally silent if she had the television and radio off.

The furnace clicking on or the refrigerator running would be loud against the stillness. She'd listen to water gurgle in the pipes sometimes or the condensation from the air conditioner drip behind the laundry, but that was it. Courtney normally filled her house with music or with the sounds of whatever show she was binge-watching, but tonight, she couldn't make herself get caught up in anything.

She was on the third season of a re-watch of the Vampire Diaries and while the show was campy and romantically thrilling, as opposed to scary, she had no desire to fuel her imagination about any sort of monster. Not even friendly vampires.

Comedy laugh tracks had sounded too loud. Any show threw odd shadows over by the window, which was now covered by a blind and had been since the neighbor's porch light had gone off and the shadows had disappeared, at least for a moment.

Courtney still didn't feel safe. She hadn't seen anyone out on the street, so it wasn't like she could go out and call to someone. She'd gone into the hall bath and listened in there. Sometimes if her neighbor played loud music, she'd hear it when she was in that part of the house, but she'd heard nothing. Just more creaking and groaning. And while she was in there, she thought she'd heard a voice, bubbling with water, call her name.

She'd barely been able to flush, she'd been in such a hurry to leave the room.

What really frightened her—though her house speaking her name, echoing through the sewer plumbing of the toilet like something out of a Stephen King novel, was scary enough—was that she was drawn to the voice.

Courtney wanted to answer the voice, to bring it into her house and talk with it about what it wanted. Except, if she did that, it could be like inviting a vampire into her home. Then she'd never be safe.

Checking her phone again, Courtney was sad to see no one had responded. She tried calling her sister this time. It was a little late to try Payton, but sometimes she carried her phone around on vibrate once her little girl was put to bed for the evening.

Once again the call didn't go through. Courtney tried looking up the weather. She was able to do that. She was also able to search Facebook to find out that lots of people in Lexington were talking about the unexpected snowfall.

Courtney had expected the snow to be widespread but it had settled around the Lexington area. Even people in Georgetown just a bit north were getting only scattered flurries. Lots of comments about how weird the snowfall was. Courtney typed in her own response but was told that she needed to be online before her comment would go through.

It surprised her because she was certain she had been online reading comments. She clicked on several threads on her timeline and she was always able to see comments. It was only when she tried communicating that her phone refused to work.

It was like something was trying to cut her off from people.

Courtney shivered. And just like that, the house groaned out her name. Again.

CHASE

Chase scratched at his arm as he waited for Cari and Julia to get ready to go out. He didn't itch so much as he felt like something was crawling on the outside of his skin, like dozens of small ants. He'd had that sensation for over a week, since before Courtney had suggested he get rid of Trag and move in with her.

The idea of being with her all the time was tempting, but he couldn't leave Trag behind.

"You took your sweet time telling her that," Trag said.

Trag's comment made Chase feel small. This was his bond-mate. He'd never had a relationship like the one he had with Trag. Trag knew what he was thinking, sometimes influencing it. He'd been changed by Trag, he knew that.

Chase had always been good at moving silently. When he was a teenager, going hunting with his father, he'd taken great pride in walking through the forest so soundlessly he could sneak up on his dad. Which had not gone over well. Once, he'd faced down the barrel of the hunting rifle. The rifle barrel had suddenly looked a lot larger than he'd expected. As the rifle had dropped, Chase had seen his father's pale face and noted the shaking arms.

He could have been killed.

Now, he could have snuck up behind the most skittish rabbit if he wanted, and in the early days of bonding with Trag, he'd wanted.

He was ready to be out in the snow. If only he hadn't traded nights with Matt then he could be out there. It was one of the things he loved about being bonded with Trag. They watched.

Chase couldn't believe he got paid to sit in a park. During the day, he'd sit under one of the trees in the small area that had been let go wild. The blue sky and green or yellow leaves would be a patchwork above him. He'd hear children laughing and the slight squeal of the swing set nearest the park entrance.

The little wooded area held plenty of squirrels to rustle leaves and birds to sing a variety of bird songs, and even a few mourning doves to hoot their haunting call. It was large enough to attract the city deer and sometimes, cloaked beneath the spell that he and Trag used to stay unnoticed, the deer would come within touching distance.

Rabbits would hurdle through the brush and pause, sniffing the air as if they almost understood that something was there. Then they'd run fleetly through the underbrush to a favorite hiding place.

Raccoons would scale the trees, their paws scratching deeply into the bark. Sometimes the squirrels would yell, disturbed by another creature making its way too close to where they lived.

The smell of exhaust would give way to the smell of damp leaves and fresh grass and sometimes the faint odor of musk when a deer got close.

Later in the summer, the cicadas would play their songs,

orchestrating a hundred or a thousand different voices into one tune, rising and falling around him.

As the day got later, the children's voices would quiet, mother's calling to take them home. The purr of cars and the occasional honk of a horn would rise as workers came home for their dinners or delivery people were out in force bringing dinner to those who worked all day.

When Chase watched at night, it was quieter. Dogs sometimes barked. He'd heard the slap of shoes on the path around the park as joggers came out in the cooler evening air. The birds would stop their songs and the cicadas would quiet.

Then it would be the frogs or toads around him croaking. In summer, lightning bugs would flash their colors around him.

The sounds of the cars would all but disappear. Sometimes it would be so quiet, he'd hear the splash of a fish in the lake behind his house. Sometimes the frogs and grasshoppers and other night creatures would make that impossible.

Owls would come out and hoot. In the evening hours after day was nearly gone and the night hadn't yet fully sunk in, the local foxes, and sometimes even a bobcat, would wander through. Early on, Chase had worried about Trag with bobcats and foxes. And then one had spotted the cat.

Trag appeared to grow bigger, the size of a broadly built doe and his fangs elongated. He let out a roar that Chase heard in his head but not in his ears. Clearly, the bobcat had heard it. He'd turned tail and run as fast as possible through the woods. Chase never worried about Trag after that.

Which was why, as soon as Julia and Cari were dressed to go out, Chase went out the front door, pausing only to catch his breath in the sudden chill that hit him. He had on a heavy jacket that had always been warm enough sitting in the park, even in the snow, but tonight it wasn't quite up to the job.

There wasn't a wind. It was like walking into a freezer naked.

He shivered. But part of him felt exhilarated.

He stepped off the long deck that lined the front of the big house and walked down the three concrete steps to the ground. He could barely make out the short walk to the driveway, though the latter was better delineated thanks to the low bushes that lined it on the side nearest the house.

The driveway was as wide as the three-car garage. It wrapped around the side by the garage so there was room for all the cars the clowder owned between them. Everyone had their own car. Drew, as the senior person in the clowder, got a spot in the garage. So did Riley. She was also senior, on her second bond-mate cat, which Chase heard was really unusual. Plus, she was older and had problems walking.

The third area was for bike storage and also held a plethora of homeowner type stuff that Chase paid little attention to.

His car was around the corner, off to the side so he could back out easily.

Julia's Subaru out front of the garage along with Tenny's Honda CRV. Chase could just make out the blue of Fin's truck from where he stood. He turned and trotted off to the portal, the snow falling around him.

The houses around him were large homes on even bigger lots. Chase thought the clowder house was ridiculously sized on a slight hill that sloped down to the lake. It included a walk-out basement and then two full floors and a partially finished attic, which was where some of the clowder had rooms.

The house next door, for instance, was also two floors in solid red brick. Two large lights designed to look like candles under glass framed the oversized two-car garage. There were four huge windows to the left of the garage and upstairs

Chase counted six windows and then two dormers up above. A huge tulip tree sat in the front, not quite centered in the yard. The tree had an unusual crook that always told Chase he was nearing the clowder house.

The streets curved oddly, and though he was good at finding his way in nature, he was less certain of himself in the city. Particularly this area of the city. It was almost as if people understood that there was something odd in at the edge of the wooded area of the park and had curved their lives around it, wanting both to avoid it and be near it.

Across the way, the white brick house with black shutters, a long, low ranch style house that was probably bigger than it seemed, had a series of black cats outlined in its front window. Halloween was coming.

Chase shivered.

"We ought to dress you up," he said to Trag.

There was no response.

Chase turned. His stomach sank. No one was behind him. In fact, as he'd walked, the street behind him had darkened. Snow came down harder, making it more difficult for him to see.

"Trag?!" Chase called, out loud this time.

Still no response. Not from Trag. Not from Julia or Cari.

STUART

It was a cold night in Columbus. You'd think he'd be used to it by now, but even after decades, he still hadn't habituated to the chill of winter in the Midwest.

Stuart longed for his home just outside Miami. He even longed for the weather of the clowder house he'd been assigned. He'd been fortunate to get a calling to go to New Mexico, to a place in the desert that was so isolated he sometimes wondered if the world had ended and it was only him and his clowder.

Things had changed since then, of course. Things do in nearly a century. After losing his bond-mate Stardust, he'd stayed in the clowder house, not certain what to do until base-command had called him, ordering him to come in. They required another worker and wanted him to consider the position.

It had sounded good at the time. There were things he hadn't known, hadn't realized. The cold and snow of Ohio were the least of them.

It was only October. Early for this kind of cold in Columbus but not unheard of. What had everyone on edge, including the command-cats, was the snow in Lexington, Kentucky.

While trace amounts to slightly measurable snow weren't unheard of, the kind of snow they were getting was more than a little unusual. Worse, the forecast hadn't called for snow or even rain when it had been broadcast that morning. By noon, there were hints of a storm brewing, something the weather forecasters were watching, puzzled, as Central Kentucky was not an area where storms suddenly appeared. Even so, the weather forecasters expected rain.

The precipitation had fallen as snow.

More snow than expected. And it was still going.

Stuart sat in his apartment, glued to his computer. His apartment had only one bedroom. His request. Stardust had whispered to him before dying that should he be tapped to continue he should always be disciplined. Stuart wasn't sure what the cat had meant and there hadn't been time to ask. Too many goodbyes and stray thoughts, memories of their time together to share in those last seconds of life.

He still wasn't certain that he understood. But here he was in a one-bedroom instead of a two or three, a falling apart old, black faux-leather sofa across the partly windowed wall that faced the gas fireplace. Stuart only ran the fireplace on the coldest days.

His one luxury was a 60-inch flat-screen television that hung above the mantle. And the computer. The computer, though…that was for work. As the youngest at base-command, it was up to Stuart to stay on top of the changing world. That meant learning computers and how to search out information from them quickly and easily.

There were others who were tasked with using computers, but Stuart knew if they needed boots on the ground, it would be up to him to go. Only a few people at base-command ever let humans see them.

Leona, in breeding, saw bond-mates when their cats came there. She had a decidedly feline way about her but she still looked mostly human. Reginald and Delores in receiving also remained human-looking. All of them had been there far longer than Stuart had been alive so he had hopes he would remain at least somewhat human for a very long time.

His boss, Darla, sounded human. Stuart knew that she didn't quite look human when you went into her office, though she used magic to create a glamor around her for outsiders and youngsters, like Stuart, who were not yet used to the strangeness of those who had been at command for a long time.

Leaving Earth and going to another world, even one they were aligned with, like Cat Home, so named because no one, except the eldest of those at Base Command, could actually pronounce the world name, changed a person. Stuart had felt the changes in his body, something changing his cells subtly, altering them forever.

He'd heard the phrase "mind-altering" but he doubted the term meant to others what it meant to him. Before, he'd been a reasonably smart guy but nothing special. Now…now, Stuart could have discussed the theory of relativity with Einstein and given him pointers. Not that he would have been allowed to. That would have been interfering.

There were physical changes, too. He was over a hundred years old and he barely looked forty.

His face had become so ordinary he could walk through a crowd of trained observers and no one would be able to describe him.

He heard cats murmuring in his mind, though he had no bond-mate. Nor could he telepathically speak to them, though he knew they could sometimes pick up his thoughts.

There were days when he picked up the thoughts of humans if they were agitated enough. He used to go out and eat dinner by himself. But as he'd aged, the thoughts became easier to read, floating into his mind almost indistinguishable from his own.

The good thing about being a computer researcher was that he could purchase what he needed online.

The building they were housed in was only a few decades old. Stuart could have designed anything for himself. A couple of people had designed entire floors. In the interest of not standing out, they had had to take half-floors.

Base-command was just outside Columbus in an area that had grown up after the building had been constructed. Ordinary people passed it every day, hardly noticing it. It was just a brick building that housed an anonymous business and had apartments above. What they didn't see was the sub-basement where the cats were bred and held until they became bond-mates in a clowder.

Stuart lived on the second floor. His computer sat on a desk in an alcove off the kitchen. Doors to the balcony were to his right. He had heavy curtains that were drawn far enough that he wouldn't feel the slight draft but open enough that he could see out in case the snow spread that far north.

Stuart had access to all the information Base Command had collected. The cats headquartered there could access certain information directly from those at Cat Home, giving Stuart access to even more background.

The problem was, that so far as Stuart could find, no cat on any world had ever encountered a creature that could come through and change the weather in such a large area.

Certain things did change the weather.

Blizzard ponies and ice dragons, for instance, would bring storms, but this was bigger than a localized storm. Even Stuart's untrained eyes could see the cloud cover building around the area of the portal in Lexington and spreading outward. He watched temperatures dropping. By midnight, Cincinnati would have snow.

If this kept up, by tomorrow night the snow would hit Knoxville in Tennessee, as well as here at Base Command.

If this was a creature capable of creating storms, it was a category five hurricane of winter storms. No blizzard pony or even an ice dragon could do that. Not unless there were many. Lexington clowder should have reported an incursion that large.

Lexington had nothing. In fact, it was rather unusual that they'd had no incursions for over a week. The last had been reported by Wilbur-bond-Matthew Logan. They'd had a small incursion of Loth worms.

It was a first for Earth, but the cats at Cat Home had records of them. The worms preferred a more sulfuric world. Stuart wasn't hopeful they'd survived the ride back without injury. There were no cats on the Loth worm world. Cat Home hadn't figured out how to create a creature that could thrive in that much sulfur. Unfortunately for the Loth worms they could have been injured and suffering before they were returned and no one would ever know.

Stuart placed a hand on his chin, thinking. The plain beige wall in front of him offered no decoration. Beside him stood a two drawer file cabinet in gray metal. A black mesh in-and-outbox rested on top of it, though the boxes sat empty.

The computer monitor was an average silver monitor that sat on a white table purchased from Ikea. Stuart had chosen the table because it was easy to set to the height he needed. Who knew how computer monitors would change in the next twenty years? With luck, he could make the table last that long.

The apartment around him was nearly silent but for the occasional thump from above. Probably water in the pipes.

The insulation between apartments was impressive. Stuart had been one of the chosen who got to walk through and inspect the work while their building was being constructed.

He smelled the usual scents of eggs and tuna and mint, which was his favorite herb. Stuart loved mint tea in the late afternoons when he settled in to watch the world outside. That and the TV were his two major luxuries. When it got cold, he allowed himself a hot rather than a lukewarm shower. Likely he'd get one of those hot showers tomorrow.

The running tab on the bottom of his screen said the cats were increasingly mentioning frost witches. Stuart didn't smile. Frost witches would be bad. They were legend only, even at Cat Home. None of the legends boded well for Earth if the cats were right.

Time dragged. Courtney thought that was the way it was in the depths of the night, as if the darkness would never end. She'd always been plagued by a fear of the dark and what might be hiding in it even as a child. Most children grew out of it. Courtney hadn't, not completely. She loved apartments and condominiums where someone was always moving and making noise so she didn't feel she had to face the dark alone

The noise of people talking, cars driving, trains honking, children thumping on floors above her lulled her to sleep. Silence, like the silence of her house, made her ears strain to hear what wasn't there. A stray thump would set her heart beating twice as fast as it should. Her palms would sweat, her mind race. She'd be awake for hours, wondering what had made the sound.

Even getting up and searching her home, a small place that didn't take much time, would have her wide awake for an hour or more at two in the morning. She missed the nights she fell into an easy sleep in her old apartment.

Tonight, in the dark, the house groaning and creaking in ways she'd not heard before, Courtney didn't think she'd ever get to sleep. If there was a blessing, it was that with the snow, chances were she wouldn't be expected at work in the morning. While the doctors and nurses might have to go, an insurance biller wouldn't be needed. She could even do calls from home if they insisted.

Of course, Courtney was one of the few people around who didn't want to work from home. She hated being alone. Or rather, she didn't mind being alone so long as there were people close by, around her, doing their own thing, because the idea of having only herself to rely on horrified her.

As a child, she'd thought she'd seen ghosts in the house. Her mom and dad lived over in the Chevy Chase part of town where homes were older than her grandparents. Their house was an elegantly redone bungalow. It had originally been two bedrooms. Her parents had finished the attic into a bedroom and a loft area with its own bathroom. The basement had been finished into a big old rec room and a laundry room. They'd even put in a half-bath down there, too.

Still, having been built in the nineteen-thirties, other people had lived in the house long before her parents. Courtney saw a sad-looking teenage girl wandering out the kitchen door on more than one occasion. She looked solid and real, almost as if someone had wandered into the house. She didn't speak. Only when Courtney followed her out to the yard and found no one there did she realize that she'd had to unlock and open the back door.

The other ghost was an old man. He always seemed angry, wandering from room to room, looking for something. Courtney had screamed the first few times she saw him, thinking he was there to take her away. Her parents had come running, but had seen nothing, even though Courtney saw them pass the man on the way to her room.

Ghosts didn't just come at night, but they seemed to show up in the silence, which was, perhaps, why she hated quietness. She'd stopped seeing the ghosts about the time she started fifth grade but she never forgot what they looked like.

Of all the people in her family, she was the most sensitive to sudden cold spots. It was one reason she avoided using her air conditioning if she could. The vents were too likely to create a natural cold spot. Cold spots reminded her of ghosts, and Courtney had no desire to find another one.

No one really understood. Until Chase.

It was something that endeared him to Courtney, why she had wanted him to move in. He'd understood that there were weirder things around than anyone expected. He'd never told her what he saw, but drew Courtney out about her ghosts.

Courtney shuddered on her sofa. She'd pulled down an orange, cream, and green afghan her sister had made. She still smelled Payton's baby powder and chardonnay scents on the yarn, years after she'd given it to Courtney. The smells made Courtney feel better even if she wasn't able to reach out to Payton.

Her big sister had been her rock.

"You know, Dad's right about the house investment," she'd said. "I know you hate being on your own like that, but your house is so close to your neighbor you could run over there and bang on the door." Payton had stood in her own gray and white kitchen, recently redone, a hand over her belly rounded with her first child.

"I can't do that at three in the morning," Courtney had said. "I won't hear them."

"You're close enough to the main road, I bet you'll hear cars and it will be fine," Payton tried to reassure her. "If you didn't want to listen to Dad, you should have purchased the condo you wanted and then told him what you did. You know how he is if you ask for his advice. If he gives it, you take it. No questions."

Courtney had laughed though she knew Payton was right. She'd listened for cars her first few nights as she'd tossed and turned. No cars. She'd tried leaving the television on but that didn't work. Her subconscious was too aware that those voices didn't belong to real people, or at least not people who were nearby.

Courtney had turned on her television after she'd cuddled down with her afghan. She watched Twilight, one of her favorite movies because it was so romantic, but she wasn't getting into it. It was a stupid choice, of course, because early on there was a hint of menace before the vampires were introduced as good, vegetarian vampires.

The romance made her miss Chase more. Courtney felt herself getting angry with him for dumping her. He could have negotiated about the cat. It was the dumbest thing. Maybe she could have given in to having a cat if she'd known it was that important. You'd think Chase would want to be out of that house with all those people. He was always talking about how he liked being alone in the woods and the mountains.

While the house had begun feeling chilly, suddenly, Courtney was warm. Too warm and she threw off the blanket, the smells that reminded her of her sister no longer pleasing. She didn't want to be reminded of her traitorous sister who had been the one to suggest getting their father's advice on the house. And then she'd said Courtney shouldn't have asked. Two-faced bitch.

Courtney wanted to scream. The heat in her body felt good. The anger felt good. It was better than being scared. The creaking and groaning in the house changed and instead of calling her name, it seemed to be laughing.

The anger drained from her, leaving her cold and scared once more. A hiss of sound came from the furnace, but whether that was a normal sound as the furnace turned off or something more sinister, she couldn't have said.

Would that night ever end?

CHASE

The night was still and silent around him. Chase didn't even hear a car driving down the main road through the subdivision. It wasn't that late. Normally there would be cars. Of course, in Kentucky, the snow would keep people in. The sounds of cars that might be out were likely eaten by the falling flakes, their ability to hush sound unmatched.

No music wafted from one of the houses. No dog barked outside, but at least that was understandable, too. As cold as it was, only the cruelest owner would send a dog out.

As the snow came down more heavily, obscuring his vision, Chase fought to see the clowder house. He was barely a house and a half away. The big red brick house next to theirs was nearly invisible in the night, the large lights on the garage the only beacon that kept him from feeling completely alone.

This was what he did best though, exist alone. He missed Trag's voice. The cat kept him from doing stupid things. Like the time Chase had been in the park under the tree. He'd used the magical cloaking that he got from Trag to sit there and watch. A young woman had been walking along the path and passed within six inches of where his feet rested in their black cross-trainers.

Chase had moved to lean forward. The girl was probably twenty or so with long blonde hair pulled back in a neat ponytail. She walked beside the path, trampling the ferns and other low growing plants when she didn't need to. Her thoughtlessness had annoyed Chase, that someone cared so little about the park. They had a concrete path for heaven's sake. He'd started to stretch his foot out, hoping to trip her.

"*Don't,*" Trag had ordered. Chase had felt his body freeze for a moment while his mind processed Trag's order, deciding whether to do it or not.

They'd argued, but the moment Chase could have tripped the annoying young woman was gone more quickly than the scent of her floral perfume, which had lingered throughout the afternoon.

Chase had to admit, that although he liked being alone, liked hiding, he wasn't thrilled to be doing it without Trag. It bothered him that he couldn't hear the cat. He hadn't realized their bond connection had been severed.

All sorts of odd explanations came to him. He'd stepped through a new portal, but he didn't think that portals just appeared. They were created and, as far as he knew, the cats or whoever bred them, made the portals appear. Maybe he'd died and not known it. He was a ghost and ghosts couldn't hear. It would be why he couldn't see much in the snow.

While Chase wasn't sure ghosts existed, his ex-girlfriend, Courtney had sworn she'd seen ghosts in her parents' house. Chase had only half-believed her, but now, if he were a ghost, he had to concede that maybe she'd been right.

Chase started back towards the clowder house. The lights faded on the big red brick house next door. The crooked tulip tree no longer guided him. He was alone in the falling snow, in a silence so thick he might have been on the moon.

The cold ate through his thick coat and the Cincinnati Reds sweatshirt he wore and then into his body. It sank through his skin, drawing his body heat out and worked its way inwards eating away at his core. The cold made it harder for his legs to move.

Chase shuffled through the snow on the sidewalk. He made out footprints going the other way, only one set. His. No one had followed him.

He didn't think that if he were a ghost, he'd be that cold. Ghosts brought cold spots but he doubted they felt them. Not that he was an expert on ghosts.

Another step, brushing the snow forward on the concrete walk. There was enough to cover the tops of his hiking boots, which were waterproof and thickly padded. He'd gone out in the snow in the mountains to do some winter hiking and his feet had never felt that cold.

It was like this cold was trying to absorb him.

Chase pushed through another step. His hips were beginning to ache. This must be how their researcher Riley felt when she complained about hip pain. He'd never been sore before. He'd always been able to count on his body to do what he needed.

As a child, he'd hunted with his father. As an adult, he camped and hiked. He disliked killing things so he hadn't gone hunting once he'd left home and his father could no longer force him to act like a man. Running track wasn't manly enough. Chase hadn't been big enough to make the football team, nor had he been interested. Track and field was perfect for him, allowing him an outlet for his athleticism without requiring the same level of team bonding that football might have required.

Feeling his hips, the ache that raised in a fever pitch

whenever he tried to move a leg was new to him. Chase had to work through it. He knew all about pushing through pain.

At the end of the driveway to the clowder house, he turned and faced a gray wall of snow and fog. He couldn't see the lights that he knew must be on in the house, both upstairs in the library and downstairs in the front room. If he couldn't hear Trag, Trag couldn't hear him. They'd be as worried about him as they were about Matt.

Unless they'd all walked out and disappeared, one after another. Chase didn't believe it. He wasn't that smart, but Amber was. She would have stopped them.

His lips felt dry. He had to force himself not to lick them. The cold would be too much for his tongue. Yet his body seemed to demand that he do it. Chase gritted his teeth.

He pushed through towards the house. Nothing. He paused midway up the drive. There were no trees, no house. It was like looking at a black hole, except, of course, the foggy emptiness was gray.

"Trag?" Chase called.

Nothing. Not in his ears. Not in his mind. He was still alone in the snow. If the clowder house wasn't there, he'd freeze to death before finding shelter, particularly as cold as he was.

Chase took another step. He scuffed the snow, noticed the concrete beneath his feet. How he could see it, he didn't know. Maybe the house wasn't actually gone.

He reached out a hand, to try and find the bushes next to the drive but they brushed nothing. He took another step. His footprints were there. His and his alone. No one else. No one had followed him.

Chase frowned.

He followed the prints, each step taking an eternity. He counted. He had to take three breathes for each step. Still, though he was moving incredibly slowly, he was moving. It was all he could do, short of lying down to die.

The thought crossed his mind. Chase pushed it away. He wasn't ready to die yet. He'd make that decision if he got to where he thought the house was and it was gone.

He was nearly to the steps when something grabbed him. Chase screamed in sudden fear. He fought.

The disadvantage was his because he couldn't see what held him. The grip on his arm felt like a hand, but he felt as if the grip was burning through his clothing and into his skin, leaving behind an aching feeling that was both hot and cold, like the menthol products he sometimes used when he overdid it. This was a thousand times more intense.

Chase's first thought was that something had come through the portal and beaten him to the house.

He let the creature pull him towards where the house had once stood. It was easier than fighting his aching hips. And the cold-hot touch felt almost good after how frozen he'd felt. Maybe that's what death was. A relief from the torments of life.

Mack was chattering at him. How Trag couldn't hear Chase. Trag couldn't even feel Chase around, like he'd walked out the door and ceased to exist. Drew knew, from things he'd heard that when a human died the cats felt as if they'd ceased to exist.

Chase had been an ass recently but he wasn't a bad guy. Drew didn't like thinking he was dead.

Drew stood out on the front porch in his heavy winter jacket, shuddering at the cold. There wasn't a wind to cut through him but the chill just seeped easily through his outerwear and ate away at him. The long-sleeved t-shirt and the flannel shirt he wore over it might have been nothing beneath the jacket. He remembered a night he'd been called out to a portal incursion when it had snowed and he'd been slightly warm dressed like that.

The lights were on in the front room. The cats, all but Trag, had stayed inside, looking out, using all their senses to try and find Chase, or at least his body. Trag would have left the porch, but Mack said Anastasia, Riley's bond-mate, had suggested he wait lest it had something to do with the snow.

Trag said he'd watched Chase step onto the first step off the porch and then he just disappeared as if he'd never been. Their bond hadn't felt severed so much as ceased to exist.

"It suggests an outside force," Mack said. *"There are creatures that can interrupt the telepathy we share, but for Trag to feel as if it was never there, that sounds like something powerful."*

Drew didn't disagree. He stood on the porch, smelling the faded, dry scent of snow that held a hint of sap from the tree in front of the house. Julia and Cari were talking, both of them huddled together, arms crossed, bouncing on their toes. Drew's feet were long since numb to the cold. They were bouncing in their winter boots.

Julia had lived in upstate New York and even she seemed cold, though her heavy puffy coat came down nearly to her knees and her boots were not only waterproofed but almost bursting with insulation. Drew envied her the clothing. Cari was dressed more like he was, except for her winter boots which didn't seem quite as up to the task as Julia's.

Fin waited just inside the door, which was only open a crack, letting some of the heat of the house out. The lights were on over the porch but it had gotten difficult to see through the falling snow. Not two minutes after Chase had left the porch, the snow had increased, as if to keep them from seeing what had happened to him.

Drew shuddered at the thought. What if there was something out there, literally eating Chase and pulling apart his body? Drew's stomach churned.

His ears strained for any sound coming from the road. While he hoped to hear Chase walking back up the drive, perhaps hear him calling, he'd be happy with the sound of a dog barking or a child laughing. Intellectually, he knew that it was late for a kid and probably too cold for a dog—even the heaviest coated dogs would be at risk in this weather, but he wanted the sounds. Ordinary sounds.

"Fortunately, we have resistance to temperature extremes," Mack said. *"I could be out there, but it would do no good. We are all in here, staying warm so we can re-warm Trag when he returns, hopefully with Chase."*

Trag's fur was raised lightly across his back, trapping air to keep him warmer, where he waited on the porch, near the stairs.

Mack had assured him of his invulnerability to weather on more than one occasion when they'd had to go out in the cold, or sometimes the heat. The cats were stronger than their normal cousins, the typical house cat.

Drew had learned a bit about the cats at Base Command as well when Mack had been chosen to breed two queens. It had been a quick three-day trip, staying in a small apartment at Base Command. It was back in the corner on the first floor, a one-bedroom place with a small kitchen and a bathroom to die for.

Drew's background was such that living in shared quarters, a room in a house, or perhaps a shared apartment was all he'd ever known. He'd grown up in a single-wide trailer on the edge of town. He knew animals and often preferred them to people. It was how he'd ended up bond-mate to Mack.

He'd been in a shelter and a guy had come in asking about their services, holding the carrier. Mack had taken one look at Drew and chosen him. The cat's mind had come flooding into his and Drew knew that they'd never be separated. He'd practically grabbed the carrier and fled, but fortunately, Mack and the person chosen to bring him around to show him off had been able to explain what was happening.

Free room and board had sounded good to Drew. He was told he could keep working at the shelter if he wanted, but as time went on, he became more insulated in the clowder house world and felt he needed to be fresh for his work there. Now, the shelter work seemed overly stressful and sad, working with cats who couldn't talk and dogs who couldn't make their owners understand their behaviors.

Drew couldn't do it any longer.

The problem was, he didn't know what he could do.

So he stood out there in the cold, hoping he could help Trag and Chase.

"I hear something," Mack said. *"It's faint."*

Julia and Cari had already stepped forward, having gotten word from their twin brown tabbies, Axel and Wheelie. Trag was no doubt the one who had actually heard something.

"Don't let them step off the porch," Mack said. *"You can try it with hands held to make sure no one disappears but the sense that Trag had about the loss of his bond with Chase bothers me. It bothers Anastasia, too. She and Riley are concerned that there might be something in the falling snow."*

Drew glanced down at his feet. There were traces of snow on the porch, but most of it had fallen from the eves or had been knocked off the front bushes by their movements onto the porch. He hoped that just touching it wasn't enough to cause a problem.

"We have not detected a problem with that," Mack assured him. *"We suspect it's an issue of the snow hitting someone as it comes down from the sky."*

Julia was leaning her upper body out into the snow, though her hood was up. She had a heavy neck gaiter pulled up over her mouth and nose. Her feet stayed on the porch, even with the overhang.

She reached out a hand and drew back. Then it was out again, "I feel something!" she yelled.

Then she was fighting with whatever was out there. Cari was pulling at her. Drew moved over and held Julia and Cari's arms while they tried to pull in whatever was out there, everyone hoping it was Chase.

Fin came out and held Cari while Drew focused on Julia. Then Tenny was at his back, ready to help.

Chase appeared from the snow. One moment they were just holding air and the next Chase landed on the porch.

"What the hell?" he asked. He looked down, staring at the concrete like he didn't quite believe he was there. Drew noted the slight bluing of his face.

"Get him in here," Amber ordered from inside the house. "It's too cold out there, and I need to examine him."

It would be her first priority to see what was going on physically. Drew grabbed Chase on one side. Tenny took the other.

Julia and Cari stood on the porch, hesitant to go in, probably because Matt and Wilbur were still out there. Drew didn't know how anyone could last out there for as long as Matt had been missing. They were going to have to face the fact that they'd probably lost one of their watchers.

Trag brushed by his feet, running towards the basement stairs, his black toes barely touching the slate tiles of the entry floor.

Chase was having a hard time moving. Drew held him up.

"You can do it," Tenny said quietly, encouraging. Drew was surprised. She'd been more annoyed with Chase than he was. After all, all the cats knew Chase hadn't told Courtney he went nowhere without Trag for at least a day. You didn't do that to your bond-mate.

Of course, Drew had never had the opportunity to have a relationship outside the clowder. It was another way he felt lost in the world.

But for that moment, he could be strong for Chase and help him down to the basement, to Amber's medic room.

COURTNEY

The house continued to laugh at her, as Courtney huddled under the blanket. Her anger no longer warmed her. The fire that had burned inside her minutes ago had flamed hot and fast and now smoldered as dying embers in her soul.

The fear made her cold. She felt as if the very air around her was trying to steal the heat from her body, leaving behind a frozen husk of flesh that held no life. And all she could do was huddle beneath the afghan.

The problem with the afghan was that it was loosely woven, warm enough for someone sitting in a house that was nearly warm enough, not a blanket for someone trapped in an industrial freezer.

Courtney tried calling her dad again. She must have a fever to feel that cold. Surely the sounds of laughter around her were just something in the attic squeaking because of the sudden change in temperature. She knew it must be that, intellectually. It was the only logical answer.

But logic didn't satisfy her. Courtney knew something else was going on. Something she didn't understand.

She needed to hear her dad's voice, telling her what kinds of settling a house would do when the weather changed so quickly. She wanted to hear him ask her mom about whether Courtney could have a fever because she was freezing even though the thermostat hadn't changed and she heard the furnace running from time to time.

He never answered his phone.

It worried her that something might have happened to him. While her parents didn't go out on workday nights very often, it was certainly possible that the power had gone out and they'd gone to a restaurant to eat. Or maybe they had gone to Payton's.

A brief flare of hot anger pushed the chill away for a moment at the thought of lucky Payton getting to feed their parents on a night like this. Probably telling them that driving was a bad idea and setting up her guest room.

Even so, if they had gone to either of those places, her dad would have brought his phone. He would have called her back. He knew she was worried about being a homeowner. Courtney thought of all the things that might have happened, from having her furnace go out to losing power to the roof caving in.

The last was the least likely, but she'd need help for any of those things. Her dad would have answered his phone.

Frozen pipes were another thing to worry about. Courtney realized she ought to let a faucet drip. Fortunately, her outside spigots were covered. Her dad had mentioned it last weekend and she hadn't wanted to forget, so she'd taken care of it. It wasn't like she often used her outside spigots. She watered haphazardly enough that her dad was talking about setting up a sprinkler system or something so her grass wouldn't completely die.

In a condo, she wouldn't have had to worry about things like that.

She stood up, worrying about her parents having gone out for food and maybe getting into an accident on the snowy roads. It wasn't as if people in Lexington were used to driving in such weather. Her dad should have been home to answer his phone after midnight.

In the kitchen, Courtney went to her stainless steel sink and turned the faucet on slightly. The faint drip sounded like "Court." Now she had the attic with its laughing creak and the faucet trying to say her name.

Courtney left the kitchen, leaving the light on. She no longer wanted to be in the dark. Maybe if she turned on all the lights, she'd drive out whatever was scaring her. Maybe with enough light, the creak and groan of the house wouldn't sound like laughter any more but like a normal house settling. Maybe the faucet would stop calling her name.

Unfortunately, the sound of the faucet dripping sounded even more like it was saying "Corrrt," once she got to the living room. Courtney shuddered.

She left the lights on in the living room and walked into the hallway. She turned on that light. She turned on the light in the bedroom she used as an office. It was tidy and neat with all her papers in order and the laptop plugged in. Mostly, she used her tablet, not the computer.

She flipped on the lights in the room she'd use as a guest room but which would currently require guests to have a sleeping bag because she had no extra bed or even a sofa. Courtney had half a mind to turn off the light and close the door. The emptiness scared her, though she couldn't put her finger on why.

She hurried out, flicking on the light in the hall bath before going to her bedroom at the back of the house. She turned on the light in the big bathroom and in the walk-in closet off the bath. Then she crawled into bed.

Courtney knew she wouldn't sleep. She still heard the

faucet calling her, "Corrrrttt." A regular call. The attic laughter still echoed.

The blankets on her bed were warmer and she pulled them up around herself. She tried her sister again. Nothing.

Then she tried her friend, Hannah, once more. She no longer cared about waking them up. They all had jobs that would be canceled because of the weather.

Still nothing.

Courtney was still alone with a house that was calling her name and laughing at her. She ought to get up and flee. Muscles tense to leave, images of dark monsters in the garage or bigger creatures dropping on the hood of her car as she fled flashed through her mind.

Undecided, Courtney sat in her bed and shivered. She didn't even notice the tears that gathered in the corners of her eyes and began to fall, surprisingly cool against the warm blankets.

STUART

Stuart yawned. It was late and he wasn't finding any information that seemed to help them understand what was going on down in Lexington. He stood up and stretched, feeling his muscles release from the position he'd held them in for the last couple of hours.

He'd been watching Lexington for a good hour before the snow started, barely at the start of what the weather forecasters had called an unusual configuration of clouds hovering over the city. His extra senses picked up on something he didn't understand. He hated the feeling of heaviness in the pit of his stomach that he could only describe as dread. Whatever this was, it was bad.

At least it was bad for him, though he had a sense this was bigger than he was.

Meditation was a good way to work through distress. Stuart let his body flow into a cross-legged position on the floor. He placed his hands on knees that laid nearly flat against the pale wood laminate flooring, the cheapest thing Base Command would let him put in.

There was the faintest chill that came from the floor. He had a room over the guest suites for when bond-mates brought their cats in to be bred. Stuart chuckled at how easily duped the bond-mates were. He'd been one of them, Stardust having to stay for kittening as well as breeding. He'd seen nothing out of the ordinary though he now knew he'd been surrounded by things he was only beginning to understand.

In fact, if he recalled correctly, he'd thought Darla was a bit standoffish but pretty. He shook his head feeling shame and embarrassment flood his body. If she had an inkling of what he'd thought…

Stuart couldn't even imagine. He probably wouldn't be there at Base Command, years after he should have been dead, probably of age-related disease, if she knew.

As he took in a deep breath, focusing on the breath, he understood that the dread wasn't for himself. He didn't care if he died. He was well aware that he'd lived longer than he should have. He was sorry for the deal with the devil he'd made for that extended life and would easily trade it away if given the opportunity.

No, the dread was about something bigger than himself. Something was coming and he didn't think he had the ability to stand between it and humanity.

A bell rang in the apartment. He hadn't been so deep in his meditation that it startled him. Still, it took him a few moments to realize it was his cellphone. It rang rarely. Almost no one used it.

Only Base Command had that number.

Stuart rose, flowing upwards as easily as his body had flowed down. Sometimes he felt as if he were made of water rather than flesh. If he were a healer, he'd ask what they'd done to his cells. They had one healer at Base Command.

Stuart had heard that it was because healers didn't deal as well with the changes they underwent. Perhaps his early ignorance of his body made it easier to accept the changes.

Everyone changed differently. The cats they saw at Cat Home, and Stuart wasn't convinced that they were necessarily in charge any more than they were here, nor was he convinced the feline body was their natural state, had mentioned it when he'd arrived. Watchers tended to change in certain ways. Guardians in others. This was mostly because of the unique talents and genetics they brought to the bonding and, if chosen, to Cat Home.

While Stuart was certain he'd understand it if someone told him, he'd not yet found anyone to explain it. The Base Command healer was the most tight-lipped of all, glaring at him when he asked questions as if the healer couldn't believe anyone would willingly want to know.

"Hello?" Stuart got to the phone, which lay on his computer desk, on the third ring. It would have been the second if he hadn't had to orient himself on what the sound was first.

"You're going to leave for Lexington in the morning. Study up on what should keep you safe. Esselyn will bond with you for the evening so you'll have moment to moment updates. She's monitoring Lexington," Darla said. No introduction. Stuart was just supposed to know who it was.

There were maybe three people he ever talked to on the cell. His boss didn't really need to introduce herself. Esselyn, of course, was one of the command cats. She was only going to bond with him for one night, though Stuart knew she could have held the bond during his entire trip if it was deemed necessary. An ordinary bond-mate cat would have to touch him. The command cats could bond with anyone in the building just by deciding they needed to do so.

"Shall I remain awake or sleep?" Stuart asked. Darla knew

his physical needs as well as he did. It was part of her job as his direct boss.

"Given Esselyn an hour, then get a few hours of sleep. We're giving you a car. It seems the most reliable right now. Planes may not be able to land in the morning if this keeps up.

CHASE

Chase let himself be taken into the house. He thought he heard Trag, but the cat was impossibly far away, like different planets far away. He'd traveled without Trag before, once to see his cousin in San Diego. Trag's voice hadn't sounded as strong but there was still a closer connection. Chase hadn't felt alone the way he did now.

Now, Trag was barely there, barely a whisper separated by large walls that Chase didn't know how to break down.

His nose twitched at the stinging smell of disinfectant. Beneath that, he caught the sweet and smoky smell of the herbs Amber used in her treatment room. They must have taken him to the medic room instead of his bedroom.

He felt cold inside, but there was something warm on the outside and he wanted to move closer to it, to soak it up. His eyelids felt heavy when he tried to raise them. His tongue was thick and surprisingly dry in his mouth when he tried to speak.

He vaguely remembered fighting arms trying to grab him, too many for a human, or perhaps just more than one human. So much of his memory was blank. Maybe he'd been rescued.

Either that or he was dying out in the snow having one wild dream. It would make sense that it was hard to hear his cat if he was dying.

Chase thought about his life. The only really good thing he'd done was work with the clowder. Before that, his dad had berated him for not being a bigger guy. His dad didn't expect him to make anything of himself when Chase hadn't been interested in working in the mine. It had still been running when he'd graduated high school.

That mine had recently closed down and when Chase's father had talked to him on the phone, Chase had borne the brunt of the old man's frustrations, as if somehow, by not working the dying mine Chase had caused the demise.

Instead, Chase had left the mountains and found his way to Central Kentucky. He'd worked mucking stables, putting himself through a program to become an electrician. After that, he'd gotten a job with a heating and cooling company. He'd thought, at the time, that while it wasn't a great life, not the dreams he'd held as a child, at least it was a steady life. Safe.

It was something he'd had in common with Courtney. They'd both gone for safe. Practical. Even when it didn't necessarily suit their longer-term desires. Courtney had no idea what else she'd do. Neither did Chase. But they both had roofs over their heads and were able to do some of the fun things they wanted, though not everything.

Then Courtney had ruined it because she hadn't wanted Trag in her house.

Had he made a bad decision not negotiating with her to take Trag?

It wasn't that Chase didn't think he couldn't be loved again but that maybe he'd made a mistake because there wasn't time for loving again. He'd felt the pull from Courtney. Something was ending when she'd suggested moving in and deep down he knew it wasn't just their relationship.

They'd been good together, though maybe a bit boring with their dual practical natures.

Now, he was going to die alone, without even his cat. What good was a telepathic cat if he couldn't even keep Chase company as he lay dying from cold and whatever else was out there?

Something touched his arm. Heat shot through his body so deeply that Chase groaned. He could still groan. That just meant whatever was touching him could keep hurting him, punishing him for his failed life, for a longer time.

Chase tried ignoring it, following the darkness around him away from the aching points in his body. The darkness drew him so that he could hide there, sleep. When he woke, if he woke, perhaps he wouldn't hurt any longer.

"Always a quitter," his dad's voice echoed in his mind.

If he died, he'd never have to hear that voice again. He wouldn't have to hear how he'd failed by not working the mines. He wouldn't have to hear how his dad thought Chase thought he was too good for them now that he lived down in Lexington. And he certainly wouldn't have to hear his father's judgment about the clowder house commune as he called it.

No, there were lots of advantages to death.

"Come on, Chase. Don't give up on me," a woman's voice said. It was further away than his dad's. It was accompanied by an ache in his feet. He tried to pull away but couldn't. Something held him down.

Chase groaned again. He just wanted to be back in the darkness.

"Don't leave me," Trag said. He was still far away but Chase could make out the words.

"You're there," Chase said.

"I've always been here. Why haven't you been answering? I thought you were brain dead or worse," Trag said. *"All those damned zombie movies you insist upon watching and I thought something had taken over your body."*

"I couldn't hear you. I thought you were gone," Chase said.

"You were wallowing in self-pity," Trag said. *"And possibly about to let yourself die because of it. I could hear you. And I am not ready to lose a bond-mate, no matter how uncaring of my feelings he might be."*

The problem with the bond-mate cats is that they often thought and acted like cats. Trag said it was an experiment of nature over nurture or something. Given that, Chase knew he'd never talk Trag out of the fact that his feelings were more important than Chase's. If there was a reason for self-pity it was having a cat talking in his head when he just wanted to lie down and die.

COURTNEY

Courtney dozed. She couldn't have said she slept. She was too aware of the sounds of the house. The furnace clicked on and off and then on again, running and running, though the temperature of the house seemed to change little. It was cool, almost cold.

With the cold reaching her arms and even her legs, covered by the heavy, warm quilt that lay across her bed, Courtney shivered. She pulled the quilt, a yellow and green log cabin pattern that Payton had made for her when she'd purchased the house. Not colors Courtney would have chosen, but even her sister never bothered to ask her what she wanted.

Or perhaps Courtney never bothered to tell her what she liked.

Yellow and green went poorly with the beige-gray walls. No doubt Courtney's parents noticed and disapproved. Green or yellow would have been more neutral colors for the house, not the brighter colors Courtney wanted. Not that anyone seemed to care what she wanted.

At the moment, though, Courtney's greatest desire was to

be warm and to be left alone by the voices in the attic and in the kitchen faucet.

She buried her head in the covers, smelling the clean scent of the fresh linen laundry detergent that she used. She'd washed it after Chase left the last time, not wanting his scent, the faint traces of cat musk, and the other smells that were uniquely Chase, in her bed to remind her what she was missing.

The noises didn't stop.

Courtney put her hands over her ears, her face buried in the quilt, making it hard to breathe. She sniffled a little, her nose running from the crying she realized she was doing.

The noises got louder.

"Just stop it!" Courtney yelled.

The house went silent.

Still.

The furnace had just clicked off as if listening to her. The house no longer creaked. The faucet drip in the kitchen barely reached her ears and when it did, it made the ordinary sounds of a drip, the slight plunk followed in the heels of another plunk. Water moving, but no names being said.

Courtney held her breath. The silence was good, but suddenly it seemed like something was waiting. She'd been found.

Her heart began to beat faster. Her hands started to sweat. She bit her lip to bite back the sobs that threatened to escape from her throat. She couldn't cry. She couldn't draw even more attention to herself.

Courtney pulled the quilt up around her shoulders and edged back to the wall behind her bed, staring at the door of her bedroom. She half expected something to walk through that door, though she had no idea what that something would be. Just that it would be awful.

She stared so long her eyes began to water.

Courtney let out a breath. She hadn't realized she'd been holding her breath, but apparently, she had. Besides, if something were going to happen, it would have happened by then.

Drawing in another deep breath, Courtney let her shoulders relax. She was still cold.

Someone banged on the front door.

Courtney about hit the ceiling when the first bang came. Once she realized what it was, she thought of her dad. Maybe he was there. She was out of bed and into the hall before she realized that her father had a key and would have come in yelling at her about all the lights.

It could be Payton, though why her sister would drive out in the snow in the middle of the night, Courtney didn't know. Hannah was equally unlikely, although given that phones were out, perhaps someone had come to check on her. Hannah wouldn't pound that hard. She'd use the bell, her finger pressed down on it until Courtney appeared.

Maybe it was Chase. The hope sent Courtney to the front door, standing on tiptoes to peer out the little peephole.

She didn't see anyone.

The pounding stopped.

Courtney pressed her ear against the door. She heard nothing. She went to the window, looking at the blinds, wondering how she could peek out without giving herself away. Her hands were still moist with sweat, a cold sweat that chilled them even further.

Shaking, she reached out a hand to pull the blind away, just a little, so that she could get a better look at who might be out there. Maybe someone had left a package, though she couldn't remember ordering anything recently.

Besides, packages didn't come that late. Even if they did, no one would knock on a door just to deliver something. There were laws.

Courtney's stomach twisted into a knot. She wanted to vomit. She wanted to scream, but the last time she'd spoken out loud, look what had happened.

Her fingers touched the faux white wood of the blind. It was smooth and cooler than usual, but the night outside was cold.

Courtney slowly pulled it back, putting her eye to the side. Her entry was empty.

No packages waited on the porch.

No spectral figure with a hand raised. No scary face to jump out and spook her further.

She breathed out, still hoping to see something in the neighborhood. Lights around garages burned though they were dim through the falling snow. The corner between Courtney's door and the garage was covered by a slight over-hang so she could see that far quite easily. However, even the house across the street had a slight blur as flakes fell more quickly than they'd fallen earlier.

Looking at her lawn, the blanket of white was thick, probably seven or eight inches already, and there appeared to be no sign of the snow stopping. This wasn't normal for October.

Courtney let the blind fall back against the window. The faint clack sounded loud in the house. It seemed to echo the way things did in an empty house, though the room was filled with furniture.

Rubbing her arms, Courtney went to head back to the bedroom.

Then the attic squeaked and groaned again. This time the voice was a whisper which came from everywhere.

"You're ours now, Courtney," it said.

Tears flowing, Courtney ran back to her bed and pulled the blanket up around her, nearly to her eyes. She picked up her phone only to find that it no longer had a charge. She'd been trying to call people for so long that it was useless.

Then, she did begin to sob, no longer caring what heard her. At that point, oblivion, even in the form of death, would be a relief.

STUART

Information came into his email overnight and Stuart read all of it before heading out to Lexington. It was less than a four-hour drive in optimal conditions. He didn't expect these conditions to be optimal. His Hyundai Sonata Hybrid worked well enough for his daily work, but with the snow, he took the Base Command car Darla had arranged for him.

It was a luxury he wouldn't have allowed himself, but he wasn't the one purchasing company cars. The Range Rover was far more car than most anyone would need. However, it was the only four-wheel-drive car they had. It was driven so seldom, it still maintained a new car smell though it had been purchased almost two years ago, something that housekeeping had apologized for profusely over the phone.

Stuart let himself sink into the camel colored leather of the front seat, cool against his body from sitting in the garage in the basement of the building. The buttons and gadgets were almost overwhelming and it occurred to him that with so many features, many of the people—if indeed they could still be called people—wouldn't be able to drive the thing. Even he was a little lost.

Luxury was something he could get used to. For just a moment he wondered if he could handle such luxuries on a regular basis and still remain disciplined. Perhaps a mattress that didn't lay on the floor or a sofa that hadn't come from a garage sale that still smelled of cigar smoke.

The relaxation in his shoulders reminded him that he wouldn't stay disciplined if he allowed himself such things. He needed to do so. For Stardust, though considering how long the cat had been gone, he often wondered why he took those words so deeply to heart.

Stuart stretched out. He'd had a decent breakfast in case he couldn't stop on the way. There was plenty of gas in the car to make it to the clowder house. As he'd eaten his breakfast, a larger one of oatmeal and eggs and bacon, he'd read through the information he'd been sent.

It was suggested that he wear several layers. Watcher Chase Anders had disappeared and lost contact with his bond-mate Trag simply by stepping out into the snowfall. This mimicked the loss of Watcher Matthew Logan and his bond-mate Wilbur. The command cats and those at Cat Home who had been contacted had suggested that perhaps it was stepping out into the snow that caused a problem.

Those inside heard their bond-mates just fine. It was only upon stepping out into the snow that their connections appeared to be disrupted. Matthew Logan still had not been found, but Chase Anders had returned, on his own, upon realizing no one had followed him out onto the street, including Trag. He was currently resting in the clowder's medic room, unconscious.

His cat had gotten through to him at one point, but the connection appeared, as the cat said, static-y. Stuart wasn't sure what to make of that. He didn't understand how a bond could have static. Either the person was there and conscious or not. It took deep unconsciousness to temporarily severe the bond.

Command had people looking up creatures who could disrupt a bond. As of the time he'd left, they hadn't found any. There were plenty that had the potential to make a human go mad and believe the bond severed, but the cats were normally able to overcome such influences. Here, it did not appear that the cats could do that. Further, it was not just the humans who felt the bond disrupted. The cats lost contact as well.

Stuart started the car, listening to the soft purr of the engine. He didn't understand exactly why engines were said to purr. They had a low rumble that was nothing like a cat's. Although this was a purely gas-fueled engine, it wasn't much louder than his hybrid.

He used the backup cameras to help him navigate out of the space. Then he got to driving, enjoying the smoothness of the ride. He couldn't say he didn't like his Hyundai. It was a perfectly fine car that handled well and was comfortable. But the Range Rover took things to a new level.

The morning was cloudy enough that little sunlight came through making it feel darker than it should have been in the early daylight. A few snowflakes hit his windshield, so tiny that at first Stuart thought they were raindrops. But the spatter was the odd-shaped spiky splatter of snowflakes. Whatever was going on in Lexington had made it north.

Darla's last missive to him had told him that he might have to destroy the portal. Stuart wasn't looking forward to being ordered to do that. He'd die destroying it, that was a given. So would the clowder. Even those who had once been clowder could be destroyed if they were still linked through the magic that had bonded them to their cats. Some people seemed to let go of the magical ties while others remained attached.

He had no desire to destroy a clowder. Stuart knew it was a possibility. It was also a possibility that he'd have to open a new portal somewhere, too. Neither of those things had happened since he'd been a part of Base Command. As far as he knew, a portal had never been destroyed on planet Earth, at least not this Earth. The last time a portal had been opened was centuries ago, although there were rumors that one was about to start in Brazil. Those had been going on since he'd started at Base Command.

Stuart felt his body getting warm even through the layers of clothing he had on. He looked around and realized there were seat warmers. As sweat began to form on his brow, he pulled over—not hard as there was only minimal traffic, the forecast suggesting heavy snow later on—and figured out how to not only turn off the seat warmers but also turn down the temperature.

He was wearing wick-away moisture long johns under khaki-colored jeans under waterproof ski pants. He also had on a long-sleeved blue t-shirt under a buttoned up flannel shirt. In the seat next to him were a fleece jacket and an outdated beige trench coat. A large black umbrella rested at the bottom of the pile, along with heavy gloves.

As the air started to cool, Stuart breathed out and began driving towards I-71 which would take him to I-75. The latter would bring him to Lexington. He didn't expect any problems until he hit Cincinnati.

It had been snowing half the night there. It hadn't been forecast until late in the evening, so Stuart expected that there would be some traffic snarls. The GPS unit in the Range Rover would tell him how to get around any long delays if needed.

It was oddly freeing to be out of Base Command. Not that

Stuart liked driving. He'd come to it later in life and it wasn't something he loved. He was old enough to remember life before cars were everywhere and he still wasn't certain he appreciated the traffic that snarled roads in the cities. Yet, here he was, feeling free at last.

Base Command had become suffocating for him. Suffocating, and at the same time lonely, as if it were sucking the humanity out of him as he watched. He couldn't even think his own thoughts there, lest the command cats listen in. They might not hear everything, but Stuart had to assume they'd hear enough to know that he wasn't quite happy.

Not that anyone seemed happy. Leona put on a good face for the bond-mates bringing their cats in for breeding. She acted happy. Stuart ate lunch with her from time to time and he knew she wasn't actually happy, not anymore. She had started joyful and curious, just like he had.

Like him, she had lost her bond-mate and been at loose ends. She'd been brought to Base Command about two decades before Stuart. They'd each come to replace someone who had died. Stuart had been too new to ask how old someone had to be to die on the job, and now it was so long ago, he hated to admit he hadn't ever known. Besides, it was best not to ask too many questions once you knew your place.

Stuart merged onto I-71. There were only a handful of other cars driving south. Across the concrete divide, he noted that more cars were going north, but not many more. Stuart couldn't remember the last time he'd seen the freeway so empty. Maybe back in the early sixties when it was still called the North Freeway, but not often since.

As the city gave way to suburbs, Stuart relaxed even further. There was definitely snow, not something he loved, but the advantage was that apparently, no one else loved it either. It wasn't yet deep enough to be a problem.

The Range Rover kept good traction. Stuart was pleased that it appeared that at least the first half of his drive was going to be easy.

He turned on the radio, deciding to indulge in some music. It wasn't as if it was a huge indulgence, either. He needed something to keep him awake.

The first station was static, which was odd. Normally housekeeping had everything set for whoever was driving one of the cars. Stuart tried again. Once more, just static. He reached out to flip through and find a station, but not a single one worked.

Frowning, he pulled out his cell phone and called Darla.

"I hope this is important," she said. She answered on the first ring. Stuart had yet to catch Darla sleeping. He wasn't even sure if she did. However, she was perpetually in poor humor, at least with him.

"The radio gets only static," he said.

"Complain to housekeeping," Darla snapped as if he were an idiot.

"No. I don't think it's the car. I think it's something else. Like the bond-mates not being able to communicate. Do we still have contact with the Lexington Clowder?"

"Yes. You would have been called back if we lost contact. That would take someone with more juice than you have to help then." Darla said the last with almost a laugh. Stuart didn't ask what she meant. He knew that by Base Command standards he was weak.

"It's something to feed to the researchers there," Stuart said. "Can you get radio in Columbus?"

Darla was silent. She probably didn't play the radio often. When she came back, "Yes. The radio here plays music, if you can call it that."

"Then it changes not far outside the city."

"Or there's something different about the car," Darla said.

"I'll contact housekeeping to find out how our building is set up to receive wireless and communications. Perhaps it's more protected on the building so there's less interference?"

"It's snowing a bit more down here too," Stuart said. "Interesting."

"I hope you continue to think so. You're the one who needs to investigate this. Right now, whether we keep that portal open is up to you and your results, do you understand?" Darla's voice went hard and slightly haunting at the end.

Stuart affirmed that he did. It was up to him to make sure the clowder got a good report. He really didn't want to die. He might not be happy any longer, but he was not willing to give up.

Stuart rested an elbow on the edge of the door and touched his forehead as he thought. It was going to be a long quiet drive.

DREW

Drew sat in the breakfast nook watching the snowfall. It wasn't falling as fast as it had last night. At the worst of it, in the light from the front porch, he'd watched swirling flakes racing to find their places on the yard. Now, they were falling slowly, gently, like a Sunday afternoon walk with the dog, provided that dog was a senior dog with arthritis.

There were fewer of them, too. Drew hoped the snow would stop soon. Bad enough that Chase was downstairs, only half-conscious, moving in and out of his ability to communicate with Trag.

"And Trag is not pleased," Mack said quietly. The big orange and white tabby, with the large round orange bullseye on his side, and the swirled stripes extending outward from it, sat on the back of the sofa in the great room a few feet away. The open floor plan allowed the two of them to see each other while Drew breakfasted on a bagel with cream cheese.

He'd considered bacon but didn't feel up to making anything more than he'd already done, not right then.

Drew had been up late helping Amber with Chase.

Someone had to make sure she was safe in the medic room and half the others were terrified of needles. Amber had studied acupuncture. She was a good match for Minnett because Amber already had concepts and theories for the type of healing the cats did. She didn't need to be broken into the weirdness of matter and energy and how sometimes working with one affected the other.

Drew finished the last of his bagel. Mack had been fed. The cat had woofed down his canned food in the room they shared. It was one of only three bedrooms on the first floor. Drew had been lucky to snag it. He'd have given it up for Riley due to her joints being so stiff and sore but she worked in the library. She was happier having a room right across from that.

He picked up his cup of coffee, straight black, the only way he liked it, and sipped. The smell might have woken his mind, but his body still felt fatigued.

It had been well after midnight before they'd settled Chase down, and Amber had felt okay going upstairs. She had a heating pad on the table which would help warm Chase. She'd done some acupuncture as well as using the special healing magic that she could access thanks to her bond with Minnett.

Drew knew that once the bond-mate cats passed, the bond-mate human frequently kept some of the talents. He was still faster than most people and had an uncanny ability to anticipate a blow. He was strong, too. He'd remain that way, to an extent, even after Mack passed. Not something he wanted to dwell on.

None of those things guided him to a new position or a new way of being useful. He envied Amber having gone to school and learned something that made her valuable to others. If he were smarter, maybe he'd have been a veterinarian, but vet schools were competitive and he barely had a two-year degree. He'd struggled to sit through the work back then.

Anson climbed the stairs from the basement. Anson had a room down there, overlooking the yard from the walk-out basement. Chase's room was down there on the other side of the basement, also looking out over the yard. Trees lined the property where it began to slope down towards their lake access. On a sunny day, they could see the lake. Between the chill that had frozen at least the top part of the lake, leaving it snow-covered, and the low gray clouds, Drew could barely make out where the lake was.

"Morning," Anson said. It wasn't too upbeat but it wasn't grouchy either.

"Morning," Drew said.

"Navy said it looks like the snow is slowing down. He's hopeful we can go out and grab Matt and Wilbur soon enough," Anson commented.

Drew noticed the wording. "Grab Matt and Wilbur" sounded like they would pick them up as if the watcher team couldn't move. Suggesting that on some level Anson worried they were dead.

Anson made himself a cup of coffee. He liked his with a bit of chocolate in it. Drew loved chocolate, but he wasn't interested in mixing it in his coffee. He'd seen Anson pick up a bottle of Hershey's syrup and squeeze out half a cup of chocolate into his mug some mornings. This morning, however, he settled for a premixed mocha from the Keurig machine.

"I don't know how he'll have survived," Drew said.

"Navy says Base Command has given us permission not to watch outside right now. The cats are attuned enough to know if something comes through. If we have to, we can go out," Anson said.

Another thing Drew hadn't known. When Mack was

active, Mack would get orders like that from Base Command and pass them on. Now the two of them were just extra weight, or maybe Drew was extra weight. Mack would always be valuable.

Drew helped Amber clean the medic room, passed her needles sometimes, helped people onto the table. When she gave herself a treatment, he'd get her comfortable after she'd needled herself.

She'd taught him to do something called cupping. She had these large rounded glass cups that were like a low wide pickle jar that he'd swirl a burning cotton ball in and then place it on her back. The fire sucked the air out of the cup and create suction. Amber said it was like working on deep tissue without quite the same level of pain.

Drew wasn't allowed to do it on anyone but Amber, though. He wasn't trusted enough for that. Maybe that's why he'd worked in shelters and as a veterinary assistant. Animals trusted him.

The problem as he saw it, was that he'd gotten a taste of what it meant to age. He might remain stronger than usual for longer, but as he got older, he would lose strength and he needed to be able to do something.

"What are your plans?" Anson asked.

"I figured I'd go down and see if Amber needed help in the medic room. Unless you need another hand out with Matt?" Drew tried not to sound too hopeful.

"I think everyone is ready to volunteer. Julia and Cari wanted to go but Tom and Tenny overrode them. Tom is stronger than either of them and Tenny matches both of them in strength and speed. If they need to carry him out of the park, they'll need people who can do it and do it quickly," Anson said. "I'd go, but I've been told to stay behind too."

Drew nodded. At least Anson had been part of the discussion.

Riley thumped her way slowly down the stairs from her second floor domain. She'd thump twice and then pause. Thump again and pause. Her hips were definitely acting up.

"Did she learn anything last night?" Drew asked Mack, mentally. He didn't want Anson to know what he didn't know, just in case Anson was privy to that information.

"No," Mack said. *"Nothing new. However, I believe there is something outside the house coming this way."* Mack stood up on the back of the sofa and turned.

Several cats came running down the stairs, a couple of thumps almost as heavy as Riley, who had paused to let them by.

Anson stood up quickly. Drew followed. Fin came out of the bedroom closest to the great room, blonde hair tousled and unkempt. He was wearing a pair of gray sweatpants and a plain white t-shirt, frowning. His feet were bare.

Anson, at least had on socks, like Drew.

Chara reached the front window first, looking out.

"It's a small silver car," Mack said. *"One of those three-door things."*

A hatchback, then. The cats weren't real good with cars having the same distrust of them that normal cats had. Drew hurried behind Anson, wondering who it could be.

Both men went to the front window, opening the blinds wide. The day was bright, despite the dark clouds, the white of the snow reflecting whatever light touched it back to the sky. The car was an older model Scion XA in dull silver. No one got out of the boxy car, though Drew made out someone sitting there.

Finally the driver's good opened.

Anson opened the door and was on the porch. "Don't get out. Stay in the car!" Anson yelled.

The person out there, a woman it seemed, continued to get out. Standing there, he recognized Chase's ex. She'd only been to the clowder house a couple of times. Too many cats, she said. Which didn't bode well for her relationship with Chase.

"That should have been a deal-breaker," Mack said.

Her hair, a pale brown, almost blonde, was messed up but not like she'd just gotten up. More like she'd been pulling at it. She was wearing sweats and a tank top. Her feet appeared bare. She didn't appear to notice the snow falling around her as she walked towards the house, ignoring Anson.

COURTNEY

Courtney watched the night move from black to charcoal gray and then to ash. She'd huddled under the covers for the last part of the night, freezing and terrified.

Her eyes felt gritty and dry and her head was muzzy. She wasn't just tired. She felt drop-dead exhausted. If the house would stop calling her name, she'd fall asleep no matter how scared she was.

Courtney still held her phone, though the screen had long since gone blank. She hadn't been able to force herself to get up to plug it in. She was fidgeting in the bed, but every time she made a move, she'd hear her name whispered through the house. No matter what the whisper said, it made her shudder. The tone had gone from a sounding as if the house were creaking and groaning out the name to a voice that resembled the high pitched scratch of fingernails on a chalkboard.

But, she needed to use her toilet. Her master bedroom wasn't huge, but it did include a nice master bath with a double sink and a large fiberglass shower. Her dad said it would up the resale value if they put in a fully tiled shower at some point. Courtney hadn't taken him up on his fix it up offer just yet. Chances were, fixing the bathroom would include him picking out dull personality-less tiles and while she couldn't say the bath had personality, at least it had possibilities.

Thinking about the way her father took over everything in her life, Courtney started getting angry again. She put her foot out from under the covers. No whispers. Good.

She padded over to the bathroom, looking at her beige-gray walls which matched the rest of the house and her dark purple towels. The bathroom needed something. Courtney could imagine dark purple accent tiles on the shower, but her father would say that was ruining the resale value of the house. Courtney felt like she was his investment property, not his daughter. It was her house, paid for with her money.

She should have made other decisions, like the condo she wanted. If she lived in a condo, she could ask her neighbors if they heard her name or if they heard their own. Or, if they heard nothing at all, they might call someone to help her.

Courtney giggled at the thought of that conversation. She washed her hands at the right-side sink in the double vanity —another plus on the resale value that she didn't need—and dried them on the plush purple towels she'd found online. Her sister thought she paid too much for them. Courtney didn't mention the price to her parents.

Her temper rose, but the anger warmed her. She no longer felt chilled, deep down in her belly. She was warm now, almost hot. She pulled off her long-sleeved shirt and tossed it on the bed. She had a tank top under it, lavender— of course—with tiny lace edging the sleeves. Her sweats were gray, though they had the blue UK on one leg.

Her stomach growled. Courtney decided breakfast would be a good idea. She went to her kitchen to fix something. The faucet still dripped. The sound annoyed her. It wasn't calling her name, at least. That was something.

She rummaged in her freezer and found a breakfast bowl thing that she ate some mornings when she wasn't in a rush. That reminded her. She'd have to tell work that she couldn't get in. Not that they'd expect her, right? The snow was piled halfway up the fence and it didn't look like a drift.

Courtney thought about her work. Gloria, the skinny older woman who worked two cubicles down and was in charge of all the billing at the clinic. Gloria always smelled of tuna fish and cigarette smoke and had five cats that she couldn't stop talking about. No matter that Courtney said she was more of a dog person, Gloria went on and on about her cats.

Courtney knew more about those cats and their hunting habits and even their frickin' shit than she ever wanted to know about a cat.

Even that irritation warmed her insides. Courtney smiled for the first time since she'd run outside to the snow. She let the breakfast bowl heat in her microwave and padded back to her bedroom to check her phone. Plugged in, she ought to be able to access her email.

She wasn't surprised to see a general notice that the business office workers didn't need to come in. Good. She wasn't going to.

Courtney felt as if she'd known she wouldn't go to work. Maybe she'd never go back. She fantasized about running away somewhere, maybe Florida. The attic whispered *"Florida?"* Like a question. Like it didn't understand that Florida was a state where the sun shone and the weather was hot even in the winter months.

"Florida, ya dumb shit," Courtney snarled. She was not in a good mood. "A place where bikinis rule and rum flows and you never have to worry about snow."

On her way out the door, Courtney felt the muzziness in her head turn to a buzzing, like a million bees were flying around inside her brain attempting to escape. It tickled and itched, but it was a deep itch that she knew she'd never reach. The intensity increased until it became painful.

Courtney bent over, hands over her ears, though she wasn't hearing a sound. She hurt. She couldn't see.

Then the buzzing went back to the early morning muzziness. She felt unduly happy with the idea of Florida but she didn't know why. She'd only ever been there once and it was too crowded for her tastes. But it was warm.

Heat flooded her body again. This time she was too hot. The microwave dinged, the two little rings that signaled she missed the first bell telling her her meal was done. But she was too hot to see to it now. She pulled at her tank top.

Florida no longer sounded like a place she wanted to visit. Besides, visiting Florida would mean leaving the snow. Courtney went to her kitchen, intending to get her breakfast. Outside the snow was slowing down. She pouted.

If it slowed too much, she might get called into work again. It was Friday. Chances were the snow would be gone by Monday. She didn't want to go to work. Idiots. She fantasized about stabbing Gloria and watching the blood run from the wounds, turning the snow from boring white to red and white striped.

Courtney smiled again. Her dad's face crossed her mind but she pushed that away. Then Chase's face. She grinned. She thought about his midnight black cat. She'd love to see red flowing from that cat.

Instead of eating her breakfast, Courtney grabbed her keys and left the house. Her feet were bare, but she didn't feel the cold of the concrete. She didn't even feel the chill in the air of the garage when she pressed the garage door opener.

The cold had felt biting the night before. Now, it was a refreshing coolness against the heat of her body.

Courtney got into her little Scion and backed out. She was going to see Chase. The snow on the roads, a pristine covering that not a single track broke, told her few people were out. They were all idiots who would pay. Soon. Very soon. And she'd take great pleasure in their demise.

CHASE

Chase was cold. He knew that he was in the medic room, that Amber had put the heat on in there, and that there was a heating pad beneath his back, but he was still cold. When he opened his eyes, the lights in the room were on low. Amber had a dimmer switch so that she could keep lights on but it wouldn't be too startling for a patient when they had to get up.

Like Chase ever wanted to be her patient. He wiggled his toes. They moved. But they were chilled. He looked down. There was a blue and black afghan over a bright blue fleece blanket covering him. The room smelled smoky sweet. Amber had been using moxa on him. It was supposed to be warming, but clearly, it hadn't worked.

Chase didn't believe in acupuncture. Bunch of bunk. Amber knew a bunch of basic first aid, which she'd learned after becoming bond-mate to Minnett so she could help the clowder. He hoped she'd stuck to real medicine when treating him, but the smoky smell suggested she hadn't.

He shuddered at the fact that he'd been too out of it to know if the cat had poked him with her tiny claws. She did that for some people when working with Amber to heal. It made Chase shudder. As much as he loved animals, loved cats, the idea of being poked, intentionally, with their nails made him shudder.

And Amber with her damned needles. He remembered aching while he'd been fighting to wake. She'd used her little acupuncture needles on him. No matter that he didn't need her. Didn't need anyone.

"Trag?" Chase thought. The cat would tell him where everyone was. He'd find out what time it was.

No response.

It was like last night. Something had clipped their communication. Chase shook his head. He had on the same clothing he'd worn out last night, minus the jacket and boots. His sleeves were rolled up. His socks weren't quite aligned correctly on his feet, as if they'd been removed and not put on quite correctly.

He leaned down to fix them. The white vinyl flooring was bright even in the dim light. He hated the medic room, not just because he hated what went on there—he knew that was necessary—but because it was sterile. White floors, cream walls, white cabinets, and a laminate counter in the palest blue. Whoever had come up with the color scheme hadn't given a thought to eye comfort.

There were three tables, the sort that raised and lowered and the head could be raised up or the area under the knee could be raised to make sure the user was comfortable. Amber had to arrange the settings, not the person on the table. It seemed unfair to Chase that he was at her mercy for comfort. Just like he was at her mercy when he was unconscious.

The tables were a dark forest green when they weren't covered over with cream flannel sheets. The cream made them blend into the cream and white room like white shadows in the snow.

Snow. The idea made him smile. Chase hurried out of the medic room into the large basement great room that sat at the foot of the stairs. It ran the width of the house, a long somewhat narrow room. The far side, where the land sloped down had a set of French doors and two windows on the right. A narrow window looked out on the left.

A pool table sat just off-center, towards the right. Three small dark wood round tables, each with two blue and white striped club chairs sat to the left. A rack of pool cues hung on one wall, next to a painting with cats playing pool. A joke, certainly. One that Chase used to find funny. It didn't seem funny that morning.

The flooring became beige carpet once he exited the medic room, the padding soft against his stocking feet. He moved silently across it. Trag raised his head from the middle club chair nearest the medic room. The black shadow startled Chase. The basement wasn't very bright that morning despite the snow.

Chase gave the cat a wave. He heard nothing in his mind.

There was something creepy about not hearing the cat that he'd been hearing in his mind for years now. He ought to feel a loss. Instead, he felt a strange sense of freedom, as if Trag had been controlling him.

The snow was still falling but softly, slowly. Upstairs, people were talking. Another day, Trag might have let Chase know what they were saying.

The snow drew him towards the windows.

Chase's hand was on the handle of the French door closest to him before he realized what was going on. He didn't intend to go out without even a pair of shoes. He shook his head, trying to clear it. He purposely backed up so that he couldn't accidentally walk outside.

Not a thought he'd had before. Chase turned.

Trag watched him, his large golden eyes wide with judgment. Chase considered killing the cat. He could squeeze the life out of him quickly. That would explain why he couldn't hear Trag. No one would know. He'd do it so fast that Trag couldn't tell the others.

Chase took a step towards the chair.

As if reading his thoughts, Trag leaped off the chair and ran up the stairs. Chase sighed.

He felt relieved. He didn't actually want to kill the cat any more than he wanted to go out into the snow. There was something very wrong with him.

Chase rested his hand on the chair where Trag had been sitting. He let his head fall forward. He closed his eyes and focused on his breathing. He felt as if his thoughts were having to pass through a swamp to get to him. They were slow. And when he couldn't think, something else took over his body.

Upstairs, the front door opened. He heard Anson yell something. Chase wondered what was going on, now. He didn't intend to go up, but by the time he knew he didn't want to be there, he was halfway up the stairs.

Courtney remembered going to get her breakfast bowl. The microwave had been signaling her that it was done. She didn't remember eating. She didn't remember driving but there she was, sitting outside of Chase's house with one leg hanging out of the car.

The house was a huge red-brick thing with a covered front porch that ran along the front of the house, almost to the end. Normally, the grass was a smooth carpet of uniform green, until fall when it came a patchwork of green shades. Today, the greens of the grass were obscured by the white of the snow. Not a footprint or paw print marred the perfection of the white, except for one small area at the foot of the stairs to the porch. Courtney frowned. She wanted to go wipe out that scar.

Bushes cuddled along the extra-wide concrete driveway, their leaves a stunning display of textures that added even more shades of green. In spring and summer, sometimes there were flowers. Courtney didn't know plants so she couldn't have named them. Those greens, too, were obscured by white.

Tall bushes, like a hedge-lined the space between the side of the house and the neighbor's yard. A smallish tree, that Courtney thought was a dogwood, held several inches of snow on its naked branches. One limb leaned down as if to touch the snow. There were low shrubs and another bare naked tree robed only in white on the far edge of the lawn.

One of Chase's weird housemates stepped out onto the porch and yelled at her. She wasn't sure what he said. She didn't care. She grabbed her keys and purse, thankful she'd at least had the sense to bring that in case she was pulled over, and got out.

Her bare feet sank into the snow. Courtney felt bad that she was messing up the purity of the covering, particularly since the flakes weren't falling that hard any longer. She had a clear view of the porch. Turning around, she had a clear view of the residential street and the houses across the way, some in a brownish colored brick, another in an orangish shade that she didn't like at all. She did like the white brick house, but today that faded away into the background of the snow. Those homes were all equally huge, mansions, really.

The people around there all had too much money. It wasn't fair that they got to surround the lake and use it. It was even private, so unless people like her, ordinary people, knew a rich person you couldn't even get close to it.

The anger at the unfairness of it all kept her warm as she walked up the sidewalk towards the house. She didn't know what she was going to say to the man on the porch. He was heavier set than Chase, but about the same age.

"Courtney," Anson said quietly.

"Is Chase around?" Courtney asked. She shouldn't have started with a question. That wasn't powerful. She should have just demanded that Chase be brought to her.

"Come inside," Anson said, gesturing. Courtney walked in. She pushed the toes of her right foot against her left heel to push off her shoes. She felt nothing. She looked down. Her feet were bare, the skin a mottled color of pinks and blues, one of her toes so dark that it was almost purple. On her walls, it might have been pretty. On her feet, the colors frightened her, though she felt too foggy to understand why.

Courtney looked up, hoping the man hadn't noticed. What was his name? There were so many and she couldn't keep everyone straight. The black woman had come down the stairs, the one with the hair shorn so short you could almost see her scalp, her skull gleaming just as darkly as the rest of her skin. They called her Tenny. Courtney remembered that.

"I need to see Chase," Courtney repeated. She wasn't asking that time.

Looking straight ahead, she noticed the cats. The dark, rounded black cat that Chase called Trag glared at her. An orange and white cat sat next to him. There were two Siamese cats, one broad and tall, the other petite and slender with a wedge-shaped head, who sat just behind Trag and his orange buddy. A calico stood on the stairs. Another black cat, this one sleeker than Trag, watched from the front room. A black cat with a long white bib down its chest and white socks on its feet appeared next to the calico.

Each and every cat glared at her. They didn't want her there. They hated her.

The hatred made Courtney mad. She hadn't done anything. The cats had stolen the love of her life. Chase would be with her now if not for the cats. She rushed towards the grouping that sat just beyond the entry, in the room Chase called the great room. She'd had dinner there once, in the breakfast nook with Chase and a couple of others.

It had only happened once. Courtney had had to pull black cat fur from her mouth three times, though she hadn't noticed it in her food. The cats had invaded the very air around her. No one was going to have to go through that again.

Someone grabbed Courtney from behind, the arms like steel bands, holding her.

Courtney pulled an elbow back, hoping to hit something vital. Her feet kicked out, hoping to find shins.

The arms didn't move. Her elbow didn't connect. Her feet brushed a pair of legs that didn't belong to her but they didn't seem to harm anyone.

The man on the porch came up to her, trying to shush her as if she were an angry child.

Courtney twisted in the heavy grasp, feeling the strain on her rib cage as she moved further side to side than her body was used to. She needed to get to the cats. She needed to kill them.

Chase appeared at the top of the basement stairs.

His eyes met hers.

Something flashed in them. Something like anger. Chase took two steps towards her and stopped. He looked back at the cats.

He took a step towards them. Courtney cheered him on. He would do the deed. Then she wouldn't have to. Chase was a hunter. They'd talked about that. He knew how to kill.

Courtney imagined the slaughter.

A big man stepped in front of Chase. He didn't raise his arms, just placed himself in front of Chase, blocking his access to the cats.

"Go downstairs, now," the big man said.

Courtney wanted to scream. The big guy was clearly softer than Chase. He might have once had muscles but there was fat on that body, too. He wouldn't be fast. Chase was very fast. And he was sneaky, too. That big guy wouldn't even see him coming.

Chase tried to push forward, but he didn't try to hit the big guy.

Courtney screamed at him.

She heard a low humming. It felt like bugs walking on her skin. She twisted and turned, trying to brush them off. The arms were still holding her like they didn't feel the bugs. How could they not feel the bugs? They were all over her body, crawling around her forearms and down to her hands, and from her elbow up to her shoulders. She felt one step onto her barefoot. Courtney shook the foot, trying to dislodge it, but the bug and its friends just kept walking up her legs.

They crawled up onto her scalp. She thought she felt one crawling into her ear. She would have shrieked again but there was one near her lip and she couldn't stomach the thought that it would get in her mouth and crawl down her throat.

The humming sound changed and Courtney realized it was the cats purring.

The realization made the crawling sensation lessen. She breathed out. Stopped struggling.

"It's working," the person behind her said.

Courtney looked down. The hands grasping her had black skin. Tenny. She wasn't a big woman but she was certainly strong.

Something in Courtney filed that away, thinking this was a good thing to have learned. As if she were going to fight Tenny at some point. Courtney was not a fighter. She couldn't even stand up for the home she wanted against her dad. She wasn't going to punch out a woman who could hold as still as a straightjacket.

The purring quieted. Courtney breathed out again. She was calmer. She was also cold. Her feet were so cold they burned on the tile floor.

"It's cold," she said quietly.

"Let's go downstairs," the guy who answered the door suggested. Tenny helped her walk into the great room. Chase wasn't there anymore, just gone, perhaps downstairs.

Courtney didn't have a choice but to continue down the stairs. It might be the wrong thing. She kind of wanted to leave, to go home and lick her wounds to try again another day, but she wasn't sure what she wanted to try again. She didn't even know how she'd gotten to the house.

That might have been the most frightening thing of all. At least it was until she got to the basement and saw the room they were bringing her to. It looked like a medical treatment room, except this was in the basement of a house. In a neighborhood. All too familiar with horror movies, Courtney tried to turn and run back up the stairs, but both Tenny and the big guy who had been with Chase, were there, blocking her path.

Courtney whimpered but let them push her into the room. They made her lie down on a table. The table was warm. The room was warm. At least if they were doing medical experiments on her, she'd be warm before she died.

Stuart felt unsettled, to say the least, driving through Cincinnati with only two other cars on the freeway with him. Herd animals, used to being shoulder to shoulder with others of their kind suddenly cut off from the group, easy prey for a predator, must feel the same way.

The long drive and the falling snow was getting to him. Too much gray and quiet. He didn't know enough about his cell to stream music through it. Stuart hadn't ever cared, but now he could have wished for some noise in the car.

At least there weren't any traffic snarls. As he thought that, he saw the red flash of brake lights ahead of him. He pushed his own brake pedal and slowed a bit. He was going ten miles below the speed limit to avoid any chance of an accident. He had no desire to be forced out of the car in this. He might have clothing to get him from the car to the clowder house, but Stuart would prefer not to test it standing out in the snow for a longer period of time.

The car up ahead abruptly made a U-turn, forcing the second car ahead of him off onto the shoulder. The second car slid up against the guard rail, sending red and orange sparks flying.

The crazy driver still had his headlights on, a glaring brightness in the gray day, making it impossible to tell what sort of vehicle it was, not that Stuart was an expert on cars.

The light raced towards him, forcing him to swerve off to the side. Not wanting to repeat the failure of the car ahead, Stuart swerved the other direction, towards the middle of the freeway. No cars sat in his way. No other herd animals to protect him from the crazy beast in their midst.

Stuart righted himself on the road, the Range Rover's tires keeping him from spinning out—that and the fact that the weather was too cold for ice to form. Small favors.

The car that had nearly hit him raced the wrong way down the freeway, attempting to hit other cars, the same way it had attempted to hit his Range Rover.

A mile later, Stuart got his shaking hands under control enough to dial Base Command.

"What now?" Darla was clearly not happy to hear from him.

"Anything on odd behavior?" Stuart asked, knowing she'd know he meant now and not in general.

"Odd behavior? Have a category? Lexington has had a run of shootings overnight. Sixteen knife attacks. Seven car accidents, which, from what I hear is only that low because there's too much snow for most people to attempt to go out. The hospitals have also had a rush on people coming in claiming to hear their house telling them to die. Which category does your odd behavior fit in?"

"A sedan of some sort made a U-turn on I-75 and tried to run into me, head-on," Stuart said.

"So car accident oddness," Darla said. She didn't ask if he were okay. That was assumed. An advantage of having gone to Cat Home was the ability of his body to heal quickly. The downside was that it only worked on ordinary wounds. Stuart had no doubt that if he were gutted by a dragon claw the wound would heal. If the dragon used magic to gut him, the healing ability might or might not work. It was the how of the wound, not what did it.

Stuart wondered if Darla would even heal from a magical wound.

"I guess." As if categorizing oddness would help. Stuart wasn't about to say anything. Base Command loved finding patterns. Those same patterns often showed the path to a solution.

"I have several items that may interest you," Darla said. Clearly, she'd made notes, just waiting for him to interrupt her again. She expected that Stuart would have himself under control enough to pay attention to what she said.

"Okay." His voice held the hint of a question that Darla would miss.

"The people we've tracked from the hospital calls appear to have all gone out in the snow with a significant portion of their body uncovered," Darla said.

"As we thought," Stuart responded.

"As we thought," Darla echoed. "No other portals have been active since the snow started in Lexington."

"Unusual," Stuart said. He thought hard but couldn't remember another time when that had happened. The snow had started nearly twenty-four hours ago. Something came through somewhere every few hours. There were too many worlds bumping and rubbing up against each other as they floated for there not to be regular incursions.

"Very," Darla agreed. "No word from Wilbur-bond-Matthew Logan since last night. Yet we have not found a severed cord."

Command cats could trace a severed cord to a deceased

bond-mate cat. The ability rarely needed to be used. Stuart did not believe he'd heard that it had ever failed.

"Is that good?" he asked, slowly, hoping Darla wouldn't get too upset with him. He turned the fan on high as the side windows began to fog up a little. It took nearly ten seconds for the window to clear and the temperature inside the car changed not at all.

Sometimes luxury was nice.

"At this time it is not bad," Darla said. "We have hope that Wilbur-bond-Matthew Logan is still alive."

Stuart let out a breath. On the far right side of the freeway an old blue truck chugged up the ramp to merge into the non-existent traffic. Stuart pulled his attention away with an effort, feeling far too grateful to see another living being on the road.

"We continue to research but everything we've found, even at Cat Home, is pointing us towards the possibility of a frost witch or perhaps frost witches," Darla continued.

"Any legends on how to get rid of one?" Stuart asked.

"Research continues," Darla said. "Finally, we have ordered the clowder in Lexington to suspend all watchers from going out. We cannot afford to lose any more cats."

Stuart acknowledged that. Naturally, they were worried about cats. Base Command was all about the cats. When had they forgotten that the cats were there to protect the humans?

CHASE

There were few moments in Chase's life when he felt truly powerful. His father appreciated physical prowess and equated that with power. His father equated using a gun to hunt deer with power. In his father's dreams, he and Chase hunted big game in Africa.

Many men might have dreamed of shooting lions, thinking they were the proverbial king of the jungle, but Chase's father wanted to be pictured with a rhino, standing over the creature with his gun, horn turned so that everyone could see it. After all, lions were just cats only bigger. Who couldn't take on a cat?

Chase was underestimated by his father in the same way the lion was. Because he wasn't built to play football and didn't have the interest, his father thought Chase was weak. He made sure his son heard about it on a regular basis.

Once, Chase had had a sister, older than he was, but she'd died. He was too young to remember exactly why, only that it had made his father hard and his mother drink. Both of them had made Chase a man who learned to hide in the shadows and avoid things rather than face them.

It was why, when he'd heard Courtney upstairs, fighting, he'd gone up, expecting to help. He knew her problem was the cats. Chase had felt uniquely qualified to take care of as many of the bond-mates as he could. He'd felt powerful as he imagined bones crunching beneath his hands. He'd have the power over the life of another and he was absolutely certain in that moment that he could do it.

Except that Drew had stood in his way and Chase had backed down. The same way he'd backed down for his father. He'd back down to his grandfather. He'd even backed down to his mother, letting her drive when she'd already started drinking.

He'd been lucky, or perhaps not, that she'd never been in an accident. Never killed anyone when she drove just a little over the limit, not even herself.

Here was Drew, a man nearly a dozen years older than he was, with his retired bond-mate standing in front of him. Chase should have been able to take him, but he'd backed down. A coward as always.

Chase knew he could take Drew. The man was soft. Out of practice. Maybe he was strong, but Chase was fast. The thing was, deep down, Chase had no desire to kill the cats. He didn't have a desire to kill anything.

Instead, he'd turned around and gone downstairs, knowing the others were bringing Courtney as soon as the purring calmed her. He should have stopped the calming spell the cats were doing, purring together. He'd felt it in his bones, noticing how his muscles loosened ever so slightly when the thought crossed his mind.

Drew had followed him down.

When he reached the bottom of the stairs, Chase wasn't sure what to do. He didn't really want to go back to the medic room. He didn't think he needed treatment. He was having spells of doing things he didn't think he wanted to do, like trying to kill the cats, but surely that wasn't that bad. It was something that would go away.

Even if it didn't, Amber couldn't do anything about it. She was an acupuncturist for god's sake, not a doctor. Not a real doctor.

She wasn't a psychiatrist. Wasn't that who you went to when something told you to do something you didn't want to do—like killing things—before they locked you up? She wouldn't be able to help.

"Maybe go settle in your room and get some sleep," Drew said. "You don't look right. Amber can treat you there."

Chase did his best not to growl at Drew. Like the asshole knew anything. The guy was a shelter worker for god's sake. He had less schooling than Chase. Idiot, though he knew stuff just because Amber was desperate for someone to help in her stupid medic room. Anyone with half a brain wouldn't go in there.

Minnett trotted quickly down the stairs. Her black fur was smooth and thick and her white feet bounced easily up and down as she went into the medic room to help.

Chase laughed. It didn't sound like him. It sounded hyena-like. Something evil and wicked. Yet he was laughing because it was funny to think of the cat with half a brain. He could pull out the other half.

Whatever was taking over his mind didn't keep Chase from noticing the look Drew gave him, the narrowed eyes, the line between his eyebrows that suggested he didn't like what he was hearing. The dumb ass didn't have a clue what Chase was thinking.

"Just a stupid thought," Chase said, waving Drew off, backing down, *again.* He walked through the big room, looking at the dull beige carpet thinking how much better it would look with blood spatter.

Chase hurried into his bedroom. It was nothing special.

None of the bedrooms were really special. When he'd become bond-mate he'd had a choice of this room, one on the first floor that tended to get cold and was an awkward shape, or he could have fixed up one of several on the third floor. The basement suited him. It felt cave-like and safe. Trag had liked it, too. Easier to get out quickly if need be, but also not right in the line of fire.

It suited both of them.

Once in the room, Chase sat on the edge of his queen-sized bed, the brown and green comforter still partly tossed back. He put his head in his hands. Something was happening to him.

Everyone would say it was the snow, but if he were honest it had started sooner. He'd been having weird thoughts, thoughts about maybe hurting Trag and now killing the cats, for a week or so.

The thoughts had started small, like maybe pulling a bit of fur to irritate the cat, then pulling his tail on "accident." Now he wanted to harm him badly enough to kill him.

Chase's felt his chest get tight and his eyes get warm. He didn't really want those things. The moment he thought them, it felt as if it were the right thing. It would be a hard thing to kill his cat, but if he didn't back down, he'd be powerful and show everyone. He wasn't sure what he'd show them.

Thinking about it, he realized the thoughts and impulses had started around the same time he'd broken up with Courtney. She'd really screwed him up. He'd not immediately said he couldn't leave Trag. Honestly, he'd never considered that he'd be asked to so he didn't even know what to say. He didn't want to scream at her because he'd thought he loved her.

Maybe this was all some odd form of depression. Like Amber could diagnose that. She'd make a big deal of it, thinking it was related to him being out in the snow. She'd insist upon doing all sorts of weird treatments on him and make him lay there while she probed at him with needles and let Minnett sink her tiny claws into his flesh, attempting to see what his aura looked like or whatever the hell the cats did.

No. Chase would take care of this on his own. He could do this. The idea of making it on his own made him feel oddly strong. He felt a small smile cross his face.

DREW

Drew smelled the sweat that poured from Courtney's body, a too-sweet scent that reminded him of rotting fruit. After talking to Chase, he'd come into the medic room. He wanted to warn Amber about Chase. Something was wrong. But then he'd found Courtney fighting Tenny, though not doing a good job of it, and he'd forgotten all about what brought him there in the first place.

The way Courtney's hands hit the air, she was like a two-year-old having a tantrum rather than an adult trying to fight her way out. Of course, having her eyes closed didn't help. Tenny was there, holding her shoulders. Amber had a hand on Courtney's knee. Now and then the knee bucked and strained against Amber's pressure.

He heard Amber using her healer voice, which normally got someone to stay still. It did not seem to work on Courtney. Looking at the tightly pressed lips and the furrows in her forehead, Amber wasn't pleased about the fact that Courtney kept fighting.

Minnett sat on the clean white counter, in front of the cotton balls and some alcohol swabs, watching. Needles were in the upper cabinet. Drew remembered once that Bess, the healer before Amber, had used restraints.

He searched in the lower cabinets back in the corner. The healers kept things that weren't used very often in there. He found a plastic box container, opened it, and found what he was looking for. The restraints were heavy leather and had a buckle on them. Not impossible to get out of, but not easy. He brought them over to Amber.

Both eyebrows went halfway to her hairline as she saw what he had.

"Bess had them. I think she had to use them once," Drew said.

Amber frowned, her teeth biting into her lower lip. She finally reached out for one and fastened it to the table. Drew took that as permission to fasten the one on the other side. Tenny moved around so that he could work more easily, never letting up on Courtney's shoulders and arms.

"Let me go!" Courtney finally screamed. The suddenness of her yelling made Drew jump. He knocked the edge of his head against the heavy table and bit back a few choice swear words. No need to agitate her further.

Standing up normally, he brought the restrains around to fasten to her wrist. Amber held Courtney's other arm. Drew wondered what the situation looked like to Courtney. She was in a strange place, probably not sure what she was thinking and people were putting restraints on her.

"I'll need to needle around her feet, too," Amber said.

"There are more." Drew had only grabbed two.

Once he got Courtney's wrist fastened to the table, he went to get two more restraints for around her ankles.

"Will they get in the way of treatment on her ankles?" Drew asked.

Tenny moved to the foot of the table and held down Courtney's ankles. Courtney was still trying to fight, but the restraints were doing their job. She continued to struggle and make loud snorting noises.

As Drew leaned down to fasten the restraint to the table, he heard a growl. It was too big to be a cat. He stopped what he was doing and looked up, careful to avoid the edge of the table. Amber had stopped too.

The growl came from Courtney's mouth. Spittle flew from her lips. She was shaking her head back and forth.

"Is she having a seizure?" Tenny asked.

"It's not like any seizure I'm familiar with," Amber said. "I wouldn't rule it out, though. I don't like it."

"Leave the restraints on?" Drew asked.

"Definitely. Keep putting them on. I don't want her falling off the table if she isn't in control."

Drew went back to work. Amber had gotten her side fastened to the table and he had his mostly done. Finishing it, he pulled his up and worked around Tenny's arms to hold Courtney's ankles still. Either she was stronger in her lower body or she was fighting hard with her legs because that took him longer to hold her down and fasten the restraints. The pale leather was dark against her too white skin, the yellow tone showing how much blue colored undertones her skin held.

Courtney's ankles felt cold to his touch, too cold. Her toes were deep purple and pink, still. As soon as Drew finished putting the restraint on her other ankle, Amber was bringing over a heat lamp that sat in the corner.

"Her feet are too cold," she said. "I don't know what she did…"

"Walked across the driveway barefoot," Tenny said. "And in a tank top."

Amber shook her head. "This is bad. I don't know why she's so susceptible or if everyone is going to be acting like this."

"Mack told me that he'd heard from Base Command that there were a lot of people with hallucinations and hearing voices," Drew said.

"Minnett said the same," Amber told him, shortly.

Tenny stood on one side of Courtney, a hand lightly on her shoulder. Drew knew that if Courtney started to fight, the pressure of that hand would increase in nano-seconds. Tenny was impressive. Though she was slightly built, she was all muscle. She was a sneaky fighter, too, but then as a smaller woman, she had to be.

With her in the room, Drew knew he wasn't needed. The table closest to the door held old blankets, the ones used for Chase. He picked those up. He folded the afghan and put it in a basket near the door. He did the same for the heavier quilt. Then he pulled the sheets off and put them in a laundry bin.

Drew found clean sheets and covered the table once again. He could do this one thing to help Amber.

"Anything I need to know?" Drew thought to Mack. He hovered near the door, hating that he was a big guy hovering, feeling more like a stalker than a bodyguard.

"Base Command is sending someone named Stuart to help us," Mack said. *"I have gotten no more updates from the cats."*

Mack made that sound like a good thing. In normal times, it probably was. Mack didn't like communicating with the command cats any more than necessary. According to him, they felt as if they were alien. He said their thoughts smelled wrong and they spoke with the wrong rhythms.

Drew had no idea how thoughts could smell, but perhaps it was a cat thing. Mack was never able to show him an example of a thought smelling.

Drew wished that he had a task. The clowder needed word from Base Command to let them know what to do. They had an outsider in the medic room because she'd come to their house and had started to rush at the cats like she wanted to hurt them. Mack was certain she did. He was backed up by all the other cats.

They also had to deal with Chase. Drew hadn't had a chance to tell Amber about him. Minnett might have known and said something. Drew frowned.

Amber was standing over Courtney, her hand on her belly, the tank-top pulled up to expose pale creamy skin. Minnett sat next to her, a paw extended. Drew could just see the tiny claws extending into Courtney's flank. Minnett's eyes were half-closed and she breathed evenly, a slight rumble that was almost a purr coming from her chest.

Amber was silent. Drew knew from experience that her eyes would be closed as she looked through Courtney's body.

Drew felt like he needed to do something, but wasn't sure what. He had a sense of waiting for something to happen, like waiting for a fight.

"That's not our job," Mack said. *"We only go in when the fight's started."*

Mack was right. That was what their job had been, retired though they might by. So why did he feel like he was waiting for something to happen with Courtney? She wasn't getting out of those restraints.

Drew was about to leave when he saw Amber stiffen and gasp. Tenny was on the other side of the table, about to grab Amber when Minnett let out a loud scream as if she were in pain.

Drew didn't hesitate. He rounded the table he'd just made up and grabbed the cat, feeling her plush fur as too soft and too cold under his grasp. He cuddled her under an arm as he ran out of the room. Someone needed to help Minnett, but without Amber, he didn't know who to go to.

This had to be a nightmare. No real-life human being went to an ex-boyfriend's house and got tied up downstairs in a room that was clearly meant for some sort of medical experimentation. Courtney's mind immediately went to all sorts of odd experiments from an injection that would force her compliance to an overlord to tiny sandworms that would slip into her ear and take over her personality as they ate through her brain.

She smelled alcohol and something sort of sweet and smoky that made her nose twitch. She had to get out of there. The lights were too bright to her eyes and she was so tired. Besides, she kept trying to move her arms and legs but they wouldn't respond.

Her grip on reality was fading. Her thoughts began to fill with holes. She'd start to think one thing and it would float away before she got to the end of the thought. Though her body struggled, Courtney shivered, wondering if something had already been done to her.

The too-bright lights and the restraints suggested the worst was yet to come. Her consciousness receded from the room. Courtney felt herself falling and when she landed, she started, her body jerking.

She opened her eyes. She was in her bedroom. The beige-gray walls greeted her. She rubbed her hands against her green and yellow quilt, smelled the fresh scent of her laundry detergent. As she sat up, thinking it was a weird dream, she smelled the scent of old bacon and eggs from the breakfast bowl she'd warmed earlier.

Courtney shook her head, frowning. It had felt so real. She was wearing her tank top and sweatpants, the tie slightly loose. The lights were on in the house, as she thought she'd left them.

Maybe she'd just gone back to bed and dreamed she'd gone to Chase's. That was how dreams worked. Courtney didn't think she'd been that tired. The house settled around her, but it sounded like normal creaks and groans. Nothing laughed at her or called her name.

Pushing the blankets aside, she didn't feel too cold.

Courtney went to the window and lifted the blind. The snow had stopped. The clouds were moving off, leaving the sky a pale, cold blue.

Swallowing, Courtney noticed her throat was dry. She padded to the kitchen. She opened a cupboard and took out one of her clear plastic cups in a purple shade that she liked. Target special, but they worked for her. Hadn't she watched that show that said her belongings should bring her joy?

Courtney smiled. The cups did.

She pushed the cold water button on her refrigerator. Her dad said she didn't need such a thing, but Courtney felt that the ice maker and water dispenser were important. Her father relented because that nice of a refrigerator would increase her home's resale value. He acted like she was going to move in a few months rather than making that house her home for years.

Courtney felt annoyed with her father. Heat rose up. Something banged at her front door. Not a normal knock but a bang. She dropped the glass, the plastic bouncing on the floor, water splattering across the gray vinyl patterned to look like tile. Something touched her toe, something hot.

Her heart began to beat faster. Courtney felt heat returning to her core. She wasn't just warm. She was hot. She walked through the kitchen doorway and something banged at the front door again. It hit hard enough that the wood pressed inward. Another hit and the door would splinter.

Courtney drew herself up and pushed against the air as if she could force the air to push back the battering ram or whatever it was at her door. It was an unconscious movement, not a movement she expected to help, more like leaning forward in a car when you wanted to go faster.

A white-colored fog of air released from her hands, surprising her. The fog spun as it shot across the living room like an arrow bent on destruction. It pierced the door of her living room, becoming hard, like the world's most enormous icicle.

Through the hole, Courtney saw not a battering ram but the black and white face of a cat the size of a human being, a large human being. The icicle had pierced the cat's ear, near its skull. The cat's mouth opened and closed. It turned its head to the side, bringing up a paw to dislodge the icicle.

Courtney put her hands over her ears listening to the cat scream in pain. It was so loud. She held her eyes closed as if that could protect her from a sound that wouldn't end. When it quieted, a little, she opened her eyes again.

She was back on the table in the weird medical room. Courtney turned her head, side to side. Only the Black woman, Tenny, stayed with her. Tenny glared at her.

Courtney tried to move her arms but they were still

restrained. From far away she thought she heard the tiniest mew. It was gone before she could latch onto where it was.

The room smelled of a sweet smoky scent. People walked around upstairs. Tenny said nothing. Courtney didn't even know what to ask. Her throat burned with dryness, feeling like she'd eaten a porcupine. She tried to lick her lips but her tongue wouldn't cooperate. It felt so hot. She felt hot.

Something was burning on her feet. Courtney raised her head far enough to see a heat lamp of sorts, the orange light focused on her toes, which looked pale and bluish despite the orange light. She thought it odd that her feet could feel so hot but somehow looked cold.

She needed to escape the heat lamp. Her body burned from the inside. Her cells seemed to contract beneath the heat, drying her out further. Soon she would be nothing but a husk.

Courtney tried to say something but the only thing that came out of her mouth was a croak.

Lexington might be the second-largest city in Kentucky but it remained small compared to other cities. It reminded Stuart of large cities in the days when he'd been a young man eager to see the world.

High rises rose twenty to thirty stories in the air. It had been a long time since a building of that height was considered a skyscraper. Traffic remained light to non-existent as he approached the city from the north. Snow covered everything. Light flakes continued to fall, spiraling slowly to the ground. They were few and far between as if the snowfall were petering out.

The square towers that huddled together around the wider sprawl of the little city hadn't been visible until he was nearly even with them. Then the clouds seemed to dissipate and the sky became mottled gray and a blue so pale it hurt to look at it. Stuart was tempted to turn up the temperature in the car given how chilly the sky looked.

Stray flakes continued to fall, outliers that hadn't gotten the memo that the clouds were passing. Snow rose over a foot on the ground. Thankfully, there'd been enough traffic as the snow started that the freeway wasn't piled quite so high. Stuart wondered if Lexington had managed to plow anything. His drive on the roads through the city could be difficult.

Fortunately, New Circle Road was a major thoroughfare and shouldn't be much worse than I-75. Of course, he had to get there, first.

Stuart wasn't used to seeing Lexington so muted by snow. Normally it was a place of green rolling hills and tall, red or orange bricked buildings. Accents of white wood abounded but when walking around downtown, if there weren't any cars, he could almost imagine himself in a city of his childhood. Today, finally, there weren't any cars. Unfortunately, time did not allow for the nostalgia of an old young man from Base Command.

Stuart finally found a radio station which was playing music, or something akin to it. At least it was noise to keep him company.

The clowder house wasn't in downtown. It was just south of that, not far from the University of Kentucky. The portal was in a park, which Stuart appreciated. He hated the portal in Paris which sat in the basement of a centuries-old building in the fourth arrondissement. The clowder had apartments above, which was convenient, but the expense was enormous and sometimes other residents noticed the incursions.

Watchers and healers had magic enough to make the incursions seem plausible without giving themselves away. A rat or perhaps a homeless person wandering in, depending upon the size of the creature. Every few years there was something more difficult, but so far, no one had been carrying a cell phone and thought to snap video of the thing, which would be harder to make disappear.

There was a time when Stuart had enjoyed going to Paris. Now, he went only for the clowder there and had no desire to return. The smells were overwhelming, the city crowded. It made him thankful that only a few big cities had portals. Lexington was big enough.

Stuart took his exit, driving carefully. The snow was piled higher once he got off the freeway, the edge of the road harder to make out. He had to drive over an overpass, so he could see the tops of the guard rail. No other drivers shared the road so at least he didn't have to worry if he wasn't quite in a lane.

The phone rang, startling him. Fortunately, he came to a stoplight, which was still working. Though the snow had to be record-setting, particularly for October, the power remained on.

"Yes?" he said upon answering.

"How far are you?" Darla asked.

"Perhaps half an hour, give or take. I'm off the freeway," Stuart said.

"You're needed. Apparently, Minnett-bond-Amber Ryan has been injured. Amber Ryan is also injured. She is attempting to heal her bond-mate, but the clowder is in turmoil. The attack was not expected," Darla said.

"How did the attackers get in?" Stuart asked. He might need to park further away and slog through the snow to the back of the house.

"It was only one attacker. She came for Chase Anders. When she appeared ready to attack the cats, she was stopped, and taken to the medic room. Due to some other unusual behavior, Amber Ryan and her bond-mate attempted to ascertain what was going on with her."

"She attacked then?" Stuart asked.

"Psychically. She was restrained on the table," Darla said. "Humans, generally, do not have the ability to psychically attack. I would suggest that you look into this one. She may be a vector for whatever is going on."

Stuart started to say something but he was talking to a dial-tone. The music came back, flooding the car with a beat that happier than what he was ready for.

The light turned green, actually, it had turned green and then red and finally green again while he'd talked to Darla. Stuart eased off the brake and continued his journey to the clowder house. Darla hadn't answered how this person knew Chase or anything that might have made her unique enough to be influenced in the way she was.

Real-time information often came too slowly for anyone's liking. He needed to get used to it. A police car cruised slowly in the other direction. The officer in the car stared at him hard enough to make Stuart fidget. He wasn't sure if the officer was influenced and considering attacking or if he were just surprised to see another car on the road.

Relief flooded him when the blue and white cruiser turned a corner and was out of his line of sight.

DREW

Drew held Minnett close to his body. Compared to Mack's bulkiness, the tuxedo cat felt small and fragile in his arms. She wasn't screaming any longer, but she didn't appear to be awake, her eyes nearly closed, the slightest film of gray between the upper and lower lids. Her right ear was sitting at an awkward angle, flattening out, but her muscles were relaxed so the ear could be a problem.

"Set her down," Mack ordered.

The basement was full of club chairs, too small for several cats to hang out together. Drew set her on the pool table. The table was covered with a heavy brown cover to keep dust and stray cat hairs off it. In theory, the cats weren't supposed to be on the table, but even bond-mates were cats.

Mack leaped up onto the table almost immediately. Boyd, Tenny's big Siamese followed seconds later as did Julia and Cari's twin brown tabbies, Axel and Wheelie. Axel was the larger of the two, though neither were tiny cats.

Immediately the cats began purring as they sat as close to Minnett as possible. Boyd even had his head resting on her back. Mack curled his head into her belly so that his breath would warm her in case she needed it. Drew wished he had the power to help heal her. Without Amber, he didn't even know what to do.

Taking Minnett had been an automatic reaction. If it had been Mack, he would have grabbed and run. Amber hadn't been able to do the same for her bond-mate, so Drew had filled in. Now he was left at loose ends. It was a bit like saving someone from a burning building but not knowing how to revive them.

"*She is stable,*" Mack assured him. "*You did the right thing. I believe Tenny has released Amber as well and she will be here soon.*"

"Should I get food?" Drew asked. Fin appeared on the stairwell, hurrying down, probably told what was happening by Chara who followed him. Fin paused, seeing Drew. Chara leaped onto the table, her smaller Siamese body, lengthening and curling around the others. She might have been a small cat, but she had a loud purr, which began to harmonize with the others.

"*I think we're okay for the moment,*" Mack said. "*Blankets and a bed, perhaps. Minnett has one beneath the desk in Amber's office that she likes. Adding blankets so she can snuggle down in there would be good.*"

"What happened?" Fin asked. "We heard…Chara isn't sure…"

"I think Courtney did something to Minnett and Amber when they were healing her," Drew said.

Tenny led Amber out of the medic room door around that moment. Amber looked up. Drew had often heard the phrase *murder in her eyes* or *if looks could kill*. He'd never experienced it before. He shuddered, wondering if it was directed at him. The thought passed as it quickly became apparent that Amber was just ready to kill anyone.

"Courtney fought back and used ice against Minnett and me. She started throwing ice spears at us. I got one near my shoulder. Minnett got it on the top of her head around her ear," Amber said.

"You mean psychically?" Fin asked. Drew wouldn't have dared.

"Do you see ice spears sticking out of my shoulder?" Amber demanded. "Of course psychically. They still did damage. My entire arm aches from the cold in my shoulder. And Minnett…"

Amber looked over at the pile of cats and nodded. "I need to work on her."

Fin didn't flinch. Good on him. Drew would have beaten himself up for a day or so after asking such a question. He'd learn long ago that he was hired muscle, not brains. He didn't ask unless he had to.

Tenny slipped silently back into the medic room to keep an eye on Courtney.

"Mack suggested I get some extra blankets and fix up the bed Minnett has in the office," Drew said. "Is that okay or would you like her in your room upstairs?"

"Here is good. I'll have access to the medic room and I can go back and see if I can't work on Courtney later. Not that I want to, but clearly she's a danger." Amber shook her head and looked down at the cats on the pool table. Paws had been stretched out across Minnett so that only her head and her flattened ear were visible.

Drew went into the medic room. He grabbed the afghan that they had used for Chase. He glanced over at Courtney. She was lying on the table, still in restraints. She wasn't moving very much. Tenny stood with her arms crossed back near the counter.

Courtney's eyes opened though they remained unfocused.

She looked towards him but Drew wasn't certain she saw him.

"Useless piece of shit," Courtney said quietly.

Her eyes closed again. Tenny was already moving towards the table in case she was needed.

Drew shuddered. He'd met Courtney once, maybe twice. He'd never spent any time around her and yet there she was, speaking to his darkest fear, the fear that he'd never find a way to be useful.

Drew frowned and took the blanket into the office, which was tucked up under the stairs. There was a weird little closet in the corner that used the awkward angle of the rise of the stairwell to its advantage. There were bookshelves across the back, which Amber had filled with her books on acupuncture and herbal medicine.

A small desk holding a closed laptop faced the door. Behind it was a black office chair. The desk had a solid wood backing so Drew had to go around and look under the desk to see the bed. He pulled that around to the side of the desk and built up the blankets. There was a water dish in the far corner of the office and he pulled that closer to the bed.

Drew looked back at it and nodded to himself.

He walked back out, noting that the cats were no longer purring.

"*What's going on?*" he thought at Mack.

"*Amber is in Minnett's energetic field. She's working to clear and warm the area where the ear attaches to the head. It is best if we pause while she works,*" Mack said.

Fin stood, arms crossed, near the stairs. He watched everything, clearly standing guard, ready to fling himself into any fight that appeared.

"This is creepy," Drew told him.

"Don't I know it. Julia said the snow has stopped, though, so she's going out to try and find Matt."

"Alone?" Drew asked. He'd offer to help if she was.

Fin smiled a little and shook his head. "Cari is going. Tom is driving. His truck was at the end of the row."

"I thought Tenny and Tom were going," Drew said.

Fin was silent for a second, and still like he was listening to Chara. Then he spoke. "Everyone wants to go. Tenny's needed here. Julia and Cari can probably help Matt."

"They'll die," Courtney yelled from the other room.

Fin and Drew looked at each other. It wasn't like they were talking loudly. Drew shuddered, worried Courtney was right.

Courtney opened her eyes and she was back in her house, in her entryway. The weird medical examination room was gone, at least for the moment. She rubbed her head, trying to remember where she might actually be. Which place was real?

Her front door was fine. Nothing was banging on it. The wood wasn't damaged from the earlier banging. The house still smelled of sausage and eggs, but it was starting to smell rotted as if she'd forgotten about her breakfast for days.

Courtney looked around at the house. She wondered how she had gotten there. The sofa was still brown, still old. It was tidy, with her sister's afghan curled in the corner where Courtney had left it the night before. The house wasn't whispering to her, wasn't calling her name, nor was it laughing at her.

Her lips still felt dry, parched. She needed water. Again, she moved towards the kitchen to get something to drink. Nothing stopped her. She eyed the front door, wondering if something would try to get inside again.

Her glass from earlier lay on its side on the floor. A few

stray droplets of water pooled on the floor. One was running into the other, slowly.

Courtney ran her hands across the surface of her granite counter. It felt cool and solid beneath her fingers. The bed had felt normal, too. She turned to look out into the backyard. The snow had stopped, but the yard was covered with more snow than she'd ever encountered in Lexington. She'd gone to Colorado with an old boyfriend who wanted to teach her to ski. There she'd been knee-deep in snow. It had snowed so much they'd only gotten one day when the lifts were open all the way to the top of the mountain.

She hadn't liked it. Too cold and too windy for her. She'd struggled to control the skis and more often than not she'd fallen on her behind because she couldn't turn and was going to too fast down the hill, completely out of control.

Courtney remembered that break-up. A more normal breakup than Chase just coming by to get his things and telling her it wouldn't work. That had been weird.

The glass on the window in the kitchen began to fog up. The glass on the French door was fine. A tingle rose up Courtney's spine. A lump, not of sorrow, but fear, lodged in her throat. She might not be a savvy homeowner but she knew this wasn't normal.

She tried to get her feet to move, to leave the room before something appeared at the window, but they refused to move. Instead, she stood there, staring at the fogged-up window as words were written in it.

"Courtney." That was all. Nothing else.

Courtney wanted to scream. Instead, she ran to her bedroom. Her phone should have been there, plugged in, charging. She couldn't find it. She remembered plugging it in before breakfast or maybe right after. Still, she remembered she'd had her phone in the bedroom. It wasn't there now.

She couldn't call anyone. She'd have to go get them.

Courtney hurried down the hallway, not caring that her feet were bare and feeling cold, and opened the garage door. Her car was missing.

She placed a fist in her mouth and looked out. The garage was colder than the house, the chill air hitting her, making her shiver.

This wasn't right. She remembered the house but she also remembered going to Chase's. She remembered being restrained in a room. It was possible that they had given her something to make her hallucinate that she was back at her home. Courtney didn't understand why anyone would do that to her but she was certain, or as certain as she was about anything, that she'd spent time restrained in a room that looked like it was set up for medical experiments.

Backing out of the garage, Courtney needed to figure out what to do. She could run to a neighbor's and bang on the door until someone answered. Maybe they would have answers.

She went to the bedroom and pulled out some socks from her dresser. She sat on the edge of the bed, pulling them on. The window in there began to fog up like the window in the kitchen. It scared her, certainly, but at least it had only written her name.

Courtney tried to control her breathing, reminding herself that nothing had harmed her last time. She could deal with the writing. It was scary. But only scary. Not deadly.

She was leaving. Just as soon as she put on the socks.

Naturally, in a hurry, distracted, the socks wanted to do anything but go on her feet. Courtney was standing just in time to see the words written on the window.

"Kill them all."

Courtney didn't even have to wonder who the writing meant. It meant the people living in Chase's house. It meant the cats that lived there. She felt eager to murder them, her hands aching to feel the neck of a human being under them while she pressed her fingers together.

As she had the thought, her nails dug deeply into her hands so hard they hurt. Courtney tried to look at them, but she couldn't bring them to her face. She blinked and she was back in the medical experiment room. Alone.

The door was closed, now. Vaguely she recalled it being open earlier. The lights were still on high. A heat lamp hovered over her feet. Instead of feeling too hot, now it felt good. Courtney laid back down. She had no idea what was going on. She was not a killer.

She knew hearing voices telling you to kill someone was a bad thing. Reading messages on non-existent fogged up windows was probably worse. It had to be. The writing wasn't real, nor were the windows, yet she got a message from her window.

Her tank top was slightly raised. Courtney felt the edge with her hand. She could move that far at least. Her body felt vulnerable with her abdomen exposed. Anyone could do anything to her like that. With her hands and her feet tied down with thick caramel-colored restraints, she wouldn't be able to stop them.

In the movies, a restraint would be loose or could be worked loose. Courtney worked at hers, but nothing happened. In a movie, there would be a scalpel within reaching distance, or just. She turned her head, looking for knives but saw nothing.

Courtney licked her lips. She really needed water. She brushed her hand against her side, trying to pull the top down over her bared abdomen. Her skin was lightly wet like she'd perspired badly. She didn't remember feeling that much of a sheen on her belly even running in the summer. Not that she ran often, but she did get out in the sun sometimes.

They must have already done something to her. Maybe whatever they gave her that made her hallucinate made her sweat. Medications could do that. Courtney struggled against the restraints. Nothing changed. She didn't have the strength to break them or loosen them.

Tears welled, making it hard to see. She struggled some more before biting back a sigh and going back to waiting to see what would be done to her next.

S tuart was nearly to the clowder house, turning off the main road that would take him into the neighborhood. Snow was piled high enough that he worried about getting stuck. No one had left their homes, going out to a grocery store or anywhere else. He'd seen one other car on the main street as he'd exited New Circle Road.

The trees all struggled under the weight of the snow, branches hanging low to the ground. One appeared to have snapped off, leaning against the trunk which had snow piled on it. The neighborhood felt too silent as if all the people had disappeared, leaving Stuart alone in a snowy dystopian nightmare.

Stuart wasn't using his windshield wipers any longer. The flakes had stopped, though the clouds were thick and looked pregnant with more precipitation. Given that the temperature was barely above zero, he had no doubt that it would fall as snow when it fell.

The park was empty. Though he was supposed to rush to the house to help the healer and her bond-mate, Stuart stopped the car and looked towards the trees that framed the portal at the far end of the park. He hadn't seen photos but supposed that there might be a parking lot in front of the park.

Posts stuck up out of the white covering, one with a dark chain attached to it. It must be a fence of some sort to keep cars from driving onto the grass. There might be a walkway just on the other side. Benches rose out of the snow, their dark wood and black metal stark contrast to the white ground.

A playground was off to one side, away from the trees, snow covering the swings and even lining the slide. The play-fort that sat to one side the roof half-buried in white.

A maroon Subaru drove slowly to the park, pulling in where Stuart thought there might be a drive and parked. Two people got out along with two cats. The bond-mates were there to search for Matt.

The driver turned to look over at him, eyes narrowed. Stuart didn't give him a wave, thinking it wouldn't help. No one sane would be out in the snow.

On the other side of the street, along that block, were two long ranch-style homes and three tri-level homes that appeared to be built in the early eighties. The way the ground sloped, Stuart figured each house had a basement that allowed people to walk out to the backyard.

A woman looked out the double front door of the house closest. The pinkish brick ranch had six windows, four on one side of the door, and two on the other. A garage sat at the far end. The porch was minimally covered, snow coming almost to the edge of the doors. The dark-haired woman stood there in baggy gray shorts and a tank top as if she were thinking about going out on a hot summer day.

Stuart felt his eyebrows pull together. The woman stepped out of the house. Her feet were covered only by red thong sandals. Her skin immediately took on a bluish cast when she stepped onto what was probably a sidewalk to the driveway. She walked quickly and purposefully towards the park.

The door to the house had been left open. A dog came close, its shaggy cream and brown nose sticking out. It opened its mouth once and backed away. The dog was smarter than the woman. A man with graying hair, tall and heavyset came out. He was in sweats and a t-shirt, his feet in tennis shoes. He followed the woman, who was, perhaps, his wife.

The man also left the door open.

Two houses down another man came out. He was younger, his dark hair fashionably cut and tousled as if he'd just woken up. The slight sheen suggested he got the look with hair gel. He had a small dark beard on his chin only, neatly trimmed. He wore a button-down shirt in pale green. It looked like cotton. His khakis were heavier than the shorts the woman wore, but still, he ought to have been in a coat. He, too, stepped out of his door and went down the three steps to what was probably a walk hidden beneath the carpet of white.

Another man followed, equally neatly dressed, though he was blonde and clean-shaven. A girl, younger than the two men, perhaps a daughter or a niece followed. She wore a long skirt, though the material did not look heavy. Her top was a white camisole tank top. Her hair was pulled back in a ponytail.

From the first house, two more young people, the children of the first couple, no doubt, came out. Stuart estimated the girl at about eleven and the boy around eight. Neither was dressed for the weather any more than the others.

More doors were opening. It was getting to be a flood of people.

The dark-haired woman who had come out of the house

first had gotten to the Subaru and she was trying to open the door.

Stuart ran through his options. He pulled on the fleece jacket but left the trench coat. It wasn't snowing just then. He left the umbrella, too. He stepped out of the Range Rover and walked over to the other car. No one paid him any attention. They didn't seem to notice the Range Rover. They were focused on the Subaru.

Inside, he saw a rounded tortoiseshell cat, her black and orange mottled body changing to orange on all her feet. She was a lovely cat and sat in the backseat. The average person would have thought she was relaxed, but Stuart noted the tension in the muscles. At the edge of his hearing, he heard the low growling purr that guardian bond-mate cats made when protecting themselves and their human.

The woman began banging on the window. The driver shrunk back. He was too late to get out and confront her. The two well-groomed younger men got there and began to try and surround the car. They didn't seem to notice Stuart.

The driver put one hand on the door, near the window. The cat leaped on his lap. Stuart wasn't surprised when the people banging on the windows pulled back, looking at their hands. A small electrical shock.

It didn't disperse the group, which was rapidly becoming a crowd. People were coming out of a lot of homes, some from around the corner and down the street. They didn't walk fast, but they all walked purposefully. An old man held the hand of a little girl. The child was dressed in a heavier coat, but the zipper wasn't zipped. The old man wore only a flannel shirt and jeans.

Interesting. Even if the guardians found Matthew Logan and his bond-mate Wilbur, they would come back to a car surrounded by people who clearly meant them ill.

Stuart considered his options. He wasn't surprised to see

one of the guardians come running. Both cats were with her. They paused a few yards away. The woman guardian held something wrapped up in cloth. Though Stuart couldn't see what it was, he knew it was Wilbur.

The other guardian probably had Matt. She'd be struggling with the man's weight. He couldn't tell if the cat was alive or dead from where he was, but they would all be seriously injured if he didn't do something.

The two cats began a battle purr. A few of the humans made faces. As the purring got louder, more of them did. Stuart knew it would hurt their ears and their heads. The goal was incapacitation.

He added his strength to the cats. One of them, a large brown tabby looked up and met his eyes. They knew who he was even if the people didn't.

More people held their heads. The woman with the cat hurried to the Subaru. She pulled open the backdoor and set the cat inside. Even then, one of the young men tried to grab the cat from her. He was easy enough to avoid, partly bent over and flailing around.

The guardian kicked out at him and he went down in the snow.

The people moved around, slowly, holding their heads, but they kept moving. At the pitch the cats had with Stuart augmenting them, they should have all been writhing on the ground.

The guardian was running back towards the trees. The two cats, both brown tabbies, Stuart noticed, held their place.

Stuart let his consciousness sink towards the ground. There was always something to draw magic from there. The ground itself was hard-packed beneath the snow and the concrete. He found no insects, no worms, nothing crawling around there. He felt a few stray bacteria living, but the ground itself felt dead.

Stuart sank deeper. What he found there was also just holding on. Something else had siphoned the very life-force from the ground. Still, the ground anchored him and he pulled energy from it to him and let it pulse outward towards the people that were nearing the car.

More of them fell. Those that didn't turned towards him, seeing him as a threat.

The purposeful walking became a fast trot towards him.

Stuart quickly jogged back to his Range Rover and slipped inside.

The engine turned over easily as the people began to surround his car. Stuart saw two women guardians pulling a third between them. Stuart stayed where he was, the car idling. He let the crowd pound on his windows until the doors to the Subaru had closed.

Even then he waited, watching the Subaru pull out of the park. It was foolish to have parked in the lot. Had they been on the street, it would have been easier to race off.

When the maroon car disappeared down the road, Stuart put his Range Rover in gear and backed slowly up. The people didn't want to move. They tried shaking the car from side to side.

Stuart used his magic to give them the light electric pulse that the cats had used earlier. It didn't make them move away but it gave him a bit of clearance so he could back up further. He eased his way out of the crowd. While the people didn't seem to notice the chill weather, they were at least careful enough about their lives to not want to get hit by his car.

After creating enough room to move forward, Stuart pulled out into the street. He cruised slowly down the road. He avoided making the turn the Subaru had made, hoping to lead the crowd away. The people continued to follow him down the street.

Two or three turned down the road to the clowder house,

following the Subaru. At least Stuart had bought the clowder some time. He continued to drive slowly like a pied piper, leading the humans away. It was too bad he didn't have a plan to lose them.

Stuart turned left and tried to decide what he was going to do. Large trees lined the streets, their branches heavy with snow. One particular tree seemed to lean out over the street. As Stuart drove beneath it the snow fell upon the car, harder than snow should have hit, even heavily packed snow.

Fortunately, the Range Rover was a heavy vehicle. A lighter car might have been damaged. A driver who didn't even have his understanding of what was happening might have flinched and driven off the road.

Stuart sped up slightly. He hoped he'd given the clowder enough time to get into the house. He needed to be off the road, soon.

DREW

Drew stood at the front window when he saw Julia's dark red Subaru barrel into the driveway, barely making the turn. He didn't know what had happened, but the speed with which everyone jumped out, he would have thought they were running from the snow. The skies were gray but nothing fell, not yet.

Kayley was by the front door, already in a heavy coat. She pulled the door open and was outside when Axel, Wheelie, and Shahanna ran through.

"They have Matt and Wilbur. They're in a bad way," Mack said. *"And they were chased out of the park."*

Mack's thoughts held things he wasn't letting Drew know. Not personal things but things that would cause Drew to slow down and ponder. Grabbing a coat from the closet that was tucked in near the stairs, Drew hurried out. If Matt couldn't walk, they'd need someone strong.

Kayley, the smallest of them, was already coming back into the house a cat cuddled in a towel close to her body. Amber would know what was happening and help. She'd be without Minnett, though. Drew would need to support her. First, he had to get Matt.

Tom, Julia, and Cari were helping Matt out of the car. His head sagged. He was dressed warmly enough but looked ragged.

Drew took one arm over his shoulder and Tom took the other. Julia slammed closed doors and locked the car.

"We were followed," Cari said. She stood towards the end of the drive looking up the street.

Drew didn't hear any cars. The day was silent except for the sound of their footsteps on the cement but the snow ate even that. Cari's voice seemed too loud in the silence, something that couldn't be eaten by the snows.

"Get inside," Julia ordered. "Just stay behind them." Drew knew she referred to him, Tom, and Matt.

Maybe the followers were on foot. It would explain the hurry with which Tom was driving.

Matt tried to move his feet and legs, but he was far too slow. His arm cut into Drew's neck and dragged him down on that side. Unfortunately, Matt was no lightweight.

Going up the steps was easier. They all had to slow down. It gave Matt a moment to move his feet with Drew and Tom as his supports.

He heard Julia and Cari running up behind them.

"They're in the driveway. There's only three of them," Cari said. "So far."

"I think a bunch followed that other guy in the car," Julia said. "Axel says he was from Base Command."

"I felt him augment the cat's magic," Tom said. "He led them away from the car."

"When he gets here, we're going to have a bunch more folks banging on the doors," Drew said.

"Isn't that why we have hurricane shutters?" Tom asked.

Kentucky didn't get hurricanes but the house had metal shutters that could be closed over the windows.

"Someone has to go out and pull them closed," Drew said. Julia and Cari broke off to work the shutters on the front. They'd have a bit more time for the back.

Matt kept walking, slowly. Tom and Drew made their way through the house. Julia pulled the door closed while she and Cari worked on the front shutters. Anson came up and grabbed a coat so that he could go help the women.

They really needed more people. Drew hurried as fast as he could, but Matt could only move so quickly.

He wondered how the other man had even survived.

"Cari found a dead fire dingo that Matt and Wilbur were huddled with," Mack said. *"No one felt it come through the portal, though. Cari said the creature was still warm when she and Wheelie sent it back."*

Drew had dealt with fire dingos in his third year in the clowder. They looked a lot like a dingo, though slightly taller. They had a tendency to burst into flames for no apparent reason, hence the name. Drew had gotten a third-degree burn on his hand when he'd sent one through. Bess, the healer before Amber, had taken care of the issue but he'd had to get back to the house first. Drew still remembered the pain that he'd been in. Even after treatment, the hand had hurt for months. It was nearly a year before he could wrap it around a hot cup of coffee without wincing.

He hadn't seen a dead one. Creatures that could survive on earth didn't often just die before being sent back. Part of what watchers did was make sure that they didn't.

"Weird," Drew said to Mack. Silent, of course, because he didn't know what Tom knew, nor was he interested in engaging in a debate.

Fin was waiting for them at the bottom of the stairs. Instead of helping, he ran up the stairs, taking them two or three at a time. Clearly, he felt he was more needed upstairs than in the medic room. Kayley had placed herself by the back door, staring out.

Drew and Tom had to turn sideways to drag Matt into the medic room. Drew was glad he'd put clean sheets on the nearest table. He had no desire to have to half-drag Matt to the far table. Amber must have lowered the table when they'd brought Wilbur in. The cat was laying on a towel on the counter, the heat lap over him. Amber hovered over the cat, only just turning to watch them bring Matt inside.

"After you get Matt settled, could you get me a carrier for Wilbur?" Amber looked at Drew as she spoke. Drew was the go-to gopher. It was his own fault in trying to be useful.

"Large or small?" he asked. There were tons of carriers around the house, just in case. He wanted to know what she was thinking.

"Larger, I think. I don't want to leave him free in case there's a problem." Amber glanced significantly at Courtney who appeared to be sleeping on the table in the middle. Drew nodded. If the same thing that happened to Chase and Courtney had happened to Matt and Wilbur, it would be a bad thing.

Without Minnett, Amber was half-blind trying to diagnose. It would be nice if Base Command sent them a healer.

"Former watcher," Mack said. *"There hasn't been a fresh healer there for decades."*

"Why?" Drew asked.

"Command cats just say no one suitable, though they've never said what suitable is," Mack said.

Drew didn't even try to get what suitable was. No doubt he wasn't.

"I think it's a good thing you aren't," Mack said.

Drew said nothing in response to that. He didn't have

time to figure out why Mack thought it was good he wasn't suitable.

Still, it was too bad the guy from Base Command—*Stuart,* Mack interjected—wasn't a healer.

Matt groaned as the table raised his upper body slightly. Amber and Tom started pulling off his outerwear which was beginning to drip. Drew noticed the blue coloring on Matt's fingers.

Amber gave him a significant look. Drew hurried out to get the cat carrier for Wilbur. At least he could do that.

CHASE

Chase curled up under the covers in his room. He'd been trying to sleep but every time he dozed off he kept seeing this ugly old field of red flowers, their heads falling to the side, the colors starting to bleed away like a watercolor image getting wet.

The image scared him and he'd startle awake, again. His room felt cold even though he was wrapped tightly in his comforter with his sweatpants and sweatshirt on. He had heavy wool socks covering his feet.

He ought to take a bath, but he didn't have a bathtub. It was one reason this particular basement room was available when he'd become bond-mate to Trag. He could shower, though, running out the hot water as he luxuriated under the spray. Then he'd have to dry off, the idea of which made him feel cold again.

Thumps and bumps came from upstairs. Louder than usual. More traffic in the house. Chase wondered what was going on.

Reflexively, he reached out to Trag.

And got nothing.

He sighed.

Chase curled back up, shivering. Maybe he had a fever. He'd been outside for a long time. Amber should have healed him of that, though. He'd been in her room.

Maybe she hadn't noticed. It wasn't like she was a real doctor. Chase started to get mad. That anger filled him with a bit of warmth. He was still cold, but not shivering.

If they had a real doctor, the doctor might have been able to fix his link to Trag. Chase knew, deep down, that such an idea didn't make sense. Nevertheless, it made him feel better to think it. It made him feel better, stronger, warmer, to think badly of Amber.

He sat up, letting the covers fall from him. The angrier he got, the warmer he got. It felt good to be angry. Chase carefully moved out of the bed. He was angry, but not stupid. Moments ago he'd been huddled shivering. He wasn't going to go running from his comfortable bed just because he was momentarily warm.

He felt okay. Standing, he was still warm enough. Angry, too.

Why would Base Command let someone like Amber become part of the clowder? She was an idealistic idiot who clearly understood nothing. He had a fever. It was probably the fever that was limiting his access to Trag. When he got better, he and Trag would be just like they were. Heck, the reason he'd not known how to tell Courtney to go to hell when she wanted him to leave Trag was probably an early symptom that he was getting sick.

The walk outside had just done him in. Chase nodded to himself.

He wondered if Base Command was sending someone. If not, maybe he could get one of the other cats to request someone from there. A real healer, maybe. A doctor. He was sick and he wasn't being treated.

Having a plan warmed him further. Chase stepped out of the room. There were people over by the medic room. Something was going on upstairs, too.

The medic room was closer. Chase crossed the big room. The cover on the pool table was slightly messed up as if someone hadn't put it back carefully. That irritated him. Cat fur might get under the cover. A big old bit of fuzz would totally mess up a shot. Idiots. Chase straightened it.

Trag looked at him from the club chair. Chase looked back at the cat.

The cat made him angry. Trag looked at him like a regular old cat and not his bond-mate. There was no half-lidded look of affection accompanied by a soft murmured conversation in his head. Trag was just there, curled in the chair, his belly looking nicely rounded, though Chase knew when the cat stood, the roundness disappeared into a lengthy body.

Chase walked towards the chair. His hand reached back rather than forward. Puzzled, Chase brought the hand forward far too fast.

Trag was faster, leaping off the chair, away from Chase. He didn't even look back as he barreled up the stairs, nearly tripping Drew as he brought down a cat carrier.

Drew paused, glaring at Chase. Then he continued into the medic room with the carrier.

"You hitting your cat now?" Kayley asked. She was small but she had a commanding voice. She stood by the backdoor, her arms folding across her chest as she watched him.

"I was going to pet him." Chase knew he sounded whiney like a kid caught out.

"You reached back like you were going to hit him," Kayley corrected. "Trag saw it. I saw it. The cats know."

The cats wouldn't trust him until someone healed him. They had no real healer, just Amber.

"Maybe if we had a real doctor, I wouldn't have this problem," Chase snarled.

Chase heard someone moving behind him. He didn't turn. Didn't want to give them the satisfaction. The anger kept warming him. He felt good when he was warm.

"Your problem isn't the lack of a real doctor," Kayley said. She'd hardly moved at all.

More thumps and movement upstairs. Chase wondered what was going on up there. Whoever was behind him smelled faintly like coffee and bacon. Chase's stomach growled. He couldn't remember the last time he'd eaten. He'd not been hungry earlier but now he was. Now he was famished. He turned, intending to go up.

Tom was there. In his face.

Chase reached out an arm, not even sure what he was planning. Tom grabbed the arm with his as if expecting Chase to throw a punch.

"What? You want to hit me now?" Tom asked.

Chase shook his head. He let his arm be brought down. Tom pushed him towards his room.

"I'm hungry," Chase said. He sounded like he was five years old. Except he never would have said that at five years old, not unless asked. Things happened when you whined in his father's house.

"We'll see to it that someone brings you something," Tom said. He didn't let Chase tell him what he wanted to eat. Something warm, savory. He thought about the roast chicken that Drew sometimes made. Thanksgiving was coming. They'd have turkey together, probably. Sometimes people went home, but if Thanksgiving happened this year, they'd all be at the house.

Deep down Chase knew that things weren't changing before then.

Chase entered his room. He noted Tom closing the door behind him.

The window drew him. Chase went to the window, looking out. The snow was higher than he'd ever seen it. He wondered if it started again if it would cover the basement windows. He could open it so easily and climb out and leave.

Chase's hands rested on the sill, near the lock to pull the window up. He could leave. It just seemed like too much trouble.

Instead, he went back to his bed and crawled in. He didn't even have the will to leave. He had no endurance for pain. He didn't have what it would take to make it if he got cold again.

Chase remembered the sound of his father berating him. Once. Twice. A third time. He put his hands up, the heat of anger draining out of him, leaving him cold again.

Something had happened to him. Deep down he knew it had happened before he'd gone out into the snow. The memory was elusive and kept sliding away from him just as he thought he had it.

The neighborhood was a maze of snaking roads, which worked in Stuart's favor. As he sped up just a little, he could go around a curve and be out of sight. The downside was that the people might wander towards the clowder house. He didn't want to go directly there, in case it led more wanderers towards the place.

The people around had been silent, like zombies, except he'd seen them breathing. He'd watched a few zombie movies. Hadn't liked them. There were too many monsters out there who could take over the mind of another creature. Zombie movies reminded him of those. And that scared him. Stuart didn't like to be scared.

The people on the street were clearly not moving of their own volition. They weren't dressed for outside. He saw hands turning blue on a few of them. They felt the cold. They just didn't care.

Stuart tried to think of a creature that could take over the mind of multiple people and create snowstorms. He couldn't think of a single one.

The closest he could come was a legend.

Frost witches.

There was nothing at Base Command on how to fight frost witches, either. The witches always won in the legends. Stuart wasn't surprised that there was a creature upon which the witches were based. However, he'd have preferred that there be a way to get rid of such a creature.

He hadn't heard that they could make people do things against their will, though. If it was in the legends, it wasn't one of the common legends.

He drove through an intersection about a block before the park and continued down the hill. His GPS showed there was a cross street that would lead to the street upon which the clowder house sat. The homes he passed were all larger than the ones on the main road, two stories at least. Some, no doubt, had basements.

Stuart finally arrived at the clowder house. The red Subaru was there, locked, the roof only partly covered with snow, the tire tracks fresh. He pulled up behind a smaller Scion, a gray thing that was poorly parked as if the person wasn't sure where the driveway was. The Scion was strangely empty of snow on the top. It must belong to the woman who had attacked the healer and her cat.

Stuart reached behind him to grab the little duffle bag he'd packed. He placed it in the front seat. On the porch, the women from the park were fighting three people, though only the guardians seemed to be effective. If the guardians weren't worried about hurting their opponents, they'd already have won.

Watching, Stuart saw one of the opponents, a woman in pajama bottoms and a sweatshirt, fall into the snow near the steps. She curled up around herself and didn't go back to the fight. Stuart hoped she wasn't hurt badly.

Silver metal shutters covered the windows behind the women. The clowder had been fitted with hurricane shutters which now covered all the first floor windows. The window on the end, past the end of the porch, with the low bush in front of it, had to have been a bitch to get to. Closing them was a smart move on the part of the clowder. Stuart would have forgotten about the shutters.

Stuart pulled out his phone and called Base Command.

"Haven't you gotten there?" Darla demanded.

"They found the watcher Matthew Logan," Stuart said.

"We heard." Darla clipped off the end of that sentence. She didn't care for his report.

"There were people around. They attacked the car the guardian driver was in. I drew them off," Stuart said.

"I knew they'd been attacked," Darla said.

"The attackers were clearly human, people who lived around the neighborhood. I saw a few come out of their homes, barely dressed, none of them dressed warmly enough for this cold," Stuart said, remembering the sucking chill that had gotten him as he'd left the Range Rover. He wasn't eager to feel that again.

"I hear." Again the clipped words.

"I think those people were taken over by something. They were working against their will or even their own good." Stuart thought of the colds and illnesses that people might catch after the stress of the chill.

"They were alive?" Darla clarified.

"Yes."

"And you don't think it was a suggestion but a takeover?" It was a good question.

"They went after me when I did magic and tried to attack," Stuart said. "They had a level of decision making that I don't think you could get in a suggestion."

"It doesn't sound that way." Darla's words came out slowly. Stuart knew his idea was leading her to places she'd rather not go. Darla was good at avoiding such things.

"I'll add this to known and observed information as we search our records and those of Cat home." Those words were punctuated by a dial tone.

Stuart put his phone in his pocket, an inner pocket where it couldn't easily fall out. Then he grabbed his other stuff and strode up the walk. The under-dressed people on the porch, still flailing around ignored him, focusing on the guardian who was continually pushing them back.

Stuart glanced back. A small group was crossing the street, perhaps having followed his car.

"More company," he said.

The guardian looked up, narrowing her eyes. "I need to keep these occupied until they get shutters up in the back."

"Can I enter?" Stuart asked, politely. He wasn't a vampire to need permission but he'd found it politic to ask that at any clowder.

"Base Command?" the woman asked. Her hair was shoulder length and she was solidly built. Not unattractive, but not the sort to catch Stuart's eye. She was a good fighter.

"I am," Stuart said. He was not actually Base Command but he was from there. It was an idiom that he'd gotten used to in the last few years.

"Suit yourself on where you go. I just hope you can help." The guardian went back to her little fight. Stuart hoped that none of the other people arriving had better skills or a weapon.

He went inside, dropping his duffle by the door. He pulled off his fleece and hung it in the closet he found off to the left. He unzipped his ski pants and removed those along with the overshoes he wore. He still had on hiking boots beneath them. He debated removing those but decided against it.

An older woman came slowly down the stairs. She'd take

a step and then pause before bringing her other leg down. Hip trouble.

"Can I help you?" she asked.

Her bond-mate should have told her he was from Base Command.

"I'm Stuart," he said.

"I know," she told him. "Riley. I'm the researcher."

So she was the one. Stuart had heard about her when Anastasia had chosen her. Few got chosen a second time. He'd expected Riley to look different, perhaps more special. Instead, she was average height for a woman, a bit on the heavy side, solidly built, as his mother would have said, with hips that boded well for an easier childbirth. Those same hips were now clearly giving Riley trouble.

"Where is everyone?"

"Fin and Anson are in back opening the hurricane shutters," Riley said. "I thought they were crazy when they installed them, here, but what do you know? We needed them. The others are in the basement. Matt was out all night and Amber is working on him. You know Minnett was injured earlier?"

Stuart nodded.

Riley went on to tell him what she knew about the attack on Minnett and Amber.

"The basement stairs?" Stuart asked when the woman paused. Fortunately, she did not talk too quickly.

"Around here," Riley said, pointing him around the corner. She led the way, following her finger which she kept out in front as if she needed it to guide her.

The basement stairs were just behind the ones Riley had just come down. Stuart eyed the gray and white kitchen countertops, the little windowed alcove off the kitchen, and the large seating area by a gas fireplace. He thought he'd seen a real fireplace in the front room. The house was all done in lightly stained hardwood with plenty of rugs.

Comfortable. Nicely appointment but not overdone. He would be tempted here but he doubted that he'd suddenly feel a need to start living in the lap of luxury.

The basement stairs were narrower than those going up. Stuart started down. Even halfway, he saw several people in the main room. The room wasn't very bright because someone had already started closing hurricane shutters across those windows.

When he reached the bottom several people turned towards him.

"Amber is around there," a short woman pointed. "She can use some help."

Stuart straightened, hoping he was up for it. Healing wasn't his forte.

Courtney had been dreaming, weird dreams of barren lands and dead flowers, always red flowers, dying. When she opened her eyes, she saw a splash of red, thinking at first it was one of the dead flowers. Then it seemed like it was a splash of blood, which made her oddly happy. Unfortunately, the red was just her imagination.

She tried to raise a hand, but it was still restrained. The door to the room she was in banged open. Courtney tensed, waiting for a mad doctor to come in and experiment on her. Instead, it was just one of the ordinary-looking guys that lived with Chase. He was dressed in ski pants and a heavy coat and he was helping a big guy with a third person between them.

The person between them looked tired, his head hanging down and his mouth slightly opened. The two men laid him on the table and the Black woman came in and started helping pull his outer clothing off. Courtney tried to watch, but it made her neck hurt to hold it at that angle.

The one guy, not the big one, kept getting in her way, giving her a perfect view of his black ski-pant clad butt. It was a perfectly ordinary butt and did nothing for Courtney. Not that anyone's would have at that point. Bondage was not something she was into.

Voices talked quickly and quietly. Amber moved into her view. She held a penlight and was looking into the man's eyes. They hadn't done that to her. At least Courtney didn't think they had. She'd been having so many hallucinations.

This, too, could be a hallucination. Of course, it seemed real with her arms tied down to the table and the smell of disinfectant and sweet smoke.

Given how real everything felt no matter where she was, it was impossible to tell when she was hallucinating. For all she knew, this could be part of a bigger hallucination. Maybe she'd gone out into the snow so under-dressed that she was in bed, at home, with a fever, dreaming these weird dreams.

A few people left and there was silence for a bit. Only Tenny and the man on the table remained. Tenny kept working on him, pulling off outer clothing.

The big guy came back with a large animal carrier. Courtney shuddered, wondering what was inside. She realized too late that he held it up at an odd angle. Chances were, nothing was in the carrier. He was bringing it to something. Something behind her head that she couldn't see.

Amber came back in and went to the table with the man they just laid down. Courtney didn't see restraints.

"What happened?" Amber asked.

There wasn't an answer that Courtney could hear. Amber moved out of Courtney's line of vision. The smell of smoke got stronger. It was sweet, like bad pot.

Courtney's throat felt hot and she bit back a cough. Everything about her body felt so dry. It would be nice if they offered her something but no one even noticed she was there. Amber walked back through the room with a cigar-like thing that had smoke coming from its tip. She waved it over the guy on the other table, concentrating on his abdomen. Then she moved to his feet.

Courtney let her eyes close. The smoke bothered them. They were dry, too. If she were at home, she'd use eye drops to make them feel better. The smell just got worse and worse. She started to cough, hoping no one would notice her. She didn't need people looking at her.

A hand on her shoulder made her eyes fly open. Tenny.

"Did you need something?" Tenny asked. Her voice was surprisingly kind for someone running what had to be an illegal medical experimentation room.

"Water?" Courtney croaked.

Tenny disappeared. Amber looked at Courtney, assessing, but didn't ask how she was feeling. Amber still held the cigar thing which still smoked. It was smaller now. Courtney couldn't wait for it to go out.

Tenny came back with a glass of water. The head of the table was raised. Tenny held the cup to Courtney's lips, letting her drink as much as she wanted. Courtney worried that if she drank too much, she'd need to pee. Who knew when they'd let her up to do that?

The big guy came back into the room. He seemed annoyed that Courtney was having a drink. Tenny took the empty glass away. She didn't lower the bed Courtney was on. Maybe Tenny would have answered Courtney's questions if Courtney had thought to ask. The big guy crossed his arms and waited just inside the door, watching Amber working on the guy on the table.

Courtney knew he was watching her as well. She hated the sensation. It kept her from closing her eyes.

Her stomach started to knot like it did before getting on a rollercoaster, the whole excitement and fear sensation. Her shoulders tensed. Courtney didn't know why. She smelled something hot that changed into a sort of acidic scent she couldn't quite place. She didn't like the smell and struggled against the bindings.

Something was out there. Something bad.

Courtney struggled hard enough that Amber returned to her side and laid a hand on her head.

"It's okay," Amber said. "We've got you restrained so you can't hurt our cats."

Courtney didn't care about the cats. She just wanted to be gone. She needed to leave. The smell was danger.

She had no idea how she knew that, didn't recognize the smell, but it felt like danger.

Like something she wasn't ready for. Courtney was reminded of dreams of being in school and realizing there was a test she hadn't studied for. The same sensation came over her.

The smell didn't get stronger while Amber stood there. It remained the same but the sense of not being ready for the danger approaching got stronger.

She struggled more against the restraints.

Although she was scared, Courtney felt her muscles relax against her will. She heard, faintly, a rumbling sound. It was like ants crawling up her spine, but she couldn't react. She closed her eyes wishing it would go away.

She needed to vomit but didn't want to make a mess. Courtney wanted to laugh that she was worried about making a mess in a place where she was tied up. She ought to take great pleasure in causing them problems.

Still, she swallowed back the sour bile that crept up her throat and gritted her teeth. The rumbling sound stopped. The ants stopped walking up her back. The danger remained. Closer than ever.

Courtney's eyes flew open again when the door opened.

A man came in, so ordinary looking she wouldn't remember the business cut of his medium brown hair the moment he left. His navy blue flannel shirt was equally nondescript. He was a spy. Or one of those creatures that could turn into anything in the horror movies of Courtney's youth.

She struggled.

That, unfortunately, drew his attention and he walked over to her. Courtney bit back a scream. That would give her away, let him know she feared him. That he held the power.

She felt his power, like magic. She couldn't have said how she knew. It was like feeling heat from a fireplace when you stood close. Except his power wasn't heat, it just made the hairs on her arms stand up. If she wasn't half lying down, perhaps those on the back of her neck would raise too.

Courtney wanted his power but knew she couldn't take it. She didn't know enough, yet. If she went to sleep, she might learn how to take it.

The idea of sleep enticed her and she closed her eyes. If this man was there to harm her, better to not know what was going on, not to feel. Blackness overtook her more quickly than sleep had ever overcome her.

This wasn't like a dream. It was like being locked in a dark closet. Courtney tried to find her way out, but it was too late. She'd already agreed to this—whatever *this* was.

Walking into the medic room, Stuart felt power rolling off the woman on the second bed. It reached out to him, examined him, tried to hide away from him, and ultimately stood to face him. Normally power didn't feel quite so sentient.

The medic room was done in cream and white and more white and if the lights hadn't been slightly dimmed, he probably would have been blinded. It was nearly as bad as the reflections from the snow outside. The man who must be Matt laid on the first table. He was struggling towards consciousness, his body chilled, though his heart still beat and his lungs still worked. Stuart noted dark spots in his aura that would need further inspection.

A large-sized beige plastic and metal cat carrier sat on the counter. He knew it housed Wilbur. Stuart felt the cat's heartbeat, strong enough that Wilbur could wait for a few minutes. The plastic prevented Stuart from seeing Wilbur's aura.

Stuart was drawn to the woman on the middle table. The power came from her. She wasn't a bond-mate, though he had the sense she was sensitive and open. Her aura, though, was dark and foggy. Stuart squinted at her even as he approached the bed. She looked at him and then away, eyes closing.

The darkness swirled around her, getting stronger. It was no longer smoky-looking. It was like a swirling watercolor of black on black. It smelled of rot, but there was something familiar in the way the power worked like he'd seen aspects of it before.

Ideas started clicking through his mind, none of them good. Stuart knew he was leaping ahead of himself. First, he had to heal the clowder, perhaps stop the snow. Then he could dwell on the familiarity of the magic that radiated from this young woman.

"Where is your other infected watcher?" Stuart asked.

"His room," the big guy said. The name Drew appeared in Stuart's mind. Yes, that would be him, with his equally large orange tabby cat, Mack.

"Anyone watching him?" Stuart asked.

"Kayley is watching that area," Drew said.

"I think Tenny and Tom are out there now," Amber said. "Julia, Fin, and Cari got most of the shutters closed and locked up." Stuart had seen the locks on them, to prevent anyone trying to attack the house from breaking through. He'd noted the young man bringing in boards to cover over the main door and solidify it.

Stuart nodded. Then he turned to Matt.

"Are you ready?" he asked Amber.

"For?" Amber asked. She seemed flustered. Stuart forgot how young she really was. She might be old enough to feel as if she knew things, maybe thirty or thirty-one, but to him, that was impossibly young. Her face was still fresh and unlined and her eyes showed an innocence that you didn't find in people much older. He certainly didn't see it in his own any longer.

"Diagnosing Matt," Stuart said.

"I thought you were a watcher," Drew said. A hint of a challenge. There was always someone, often more than one, in the clowders who didn't like him. It had been easier earlier on. They appeared less threatened. As he aged and changed, Stuart found there were more challenges, as if the very alienness of his being triggered something primal.

"I was," Stuart said. "My talents changed upon going to work for Base Command. I can watch while Amber diagnoses and lend her strength, not unlike the role Minnett would play if she were not injured."

Amber nodded. Drew frowned. His arms remained crossed, not satisfied with the answer but not willing to say anything else.

Stuart took Amber's hand when she got closer to the table and to him. She looked startled, her soft hazel eyes, widening. Amber looked back at Matt, placing her hand on his abdomen, not bothering to raise his shirt. She was powerful if she could scan and sense and perhaps even heal through clothing.

Stuart let his gaze soften, following Amber's lead, lending her his power. He watched over her shoulder. Matt was deeply chilled, his organs sluggish, but it was mostly a normal chill. As Amber moved into the more energetic plane, he started seeing signs of shadows. They were pale shadows, outlines of iciness around the organs. It wasn't an internal cold that Matt would feel, but an energetic cold that would slow his reflexes and his thinking.

Amber floated through the energetic body, looking at the spine, which seemed to be entwined with dark hairs that fluttered around. In the physical world, they'd look like nerves. They shouldn't be visible there. But they were. Amber didn't touch them but dove in closer.

Stuart noticed that the hairs appeared to breathe. The movements were in reaction to the flow of energy up and down the spinal column. This close Stuart got the sense that the tendrils were alive. One paused its movements and held its endpoint towards them as if studying them.

As Amber moved on, apparently not aware of what Stuart sensed, the tendril went back to moving about. The tendrils weren't linked together or to anything in Matt's body. They were slightly wrapped around the spine but loosely, just enough to keep from floating away. They stopped about halfway up his back. His upper body was clear but for the iciness that surrounded his lungs.

Amber continued on, checking his brain, which looked normal. She slid back down the spine, but too fast for Stuart to get any real sense of what he was seeing, and down into the shadowy areas of Matt's lower body.

Once there, she pulled herself out, entering the physical realm, giving Stuart another look at the physical body, where he noted, quickly, that the spine appeared undamaged by the energetic tendrils. Then, they were out, hovering above the body.

Stuart dropped Amber's hand as things returned to normal.

"The tendrils in his spine felt alive," he said.

"I just saw them as shadows," Amber said.

Stuart shook his head. Amber bit her lip. She didn't say anything for a moment, perhaps checking in with Minnett. Stuart felt the healer cat's energy around them. She might be hurt, but she was a powerful little thing. Amber began nodding her head.

"Minnett said she was following with me and she saw something similar to what you described. I'd have seen it if she were here, but she's not quite up to using her own energy yet," Amber said. The last was a sort of apology.

"Let's let Matt rest. I want to check Wilbur," Stuart said.

The beige carrier was large and there was a heat lamp near it to help warm the cat. Stuart looked inside. Wilbur was all black, like every watcher cat he'd met. Even Wilbur's nose and toe pads were black. Stuart noticed a pink line on the lower lip as if someone had put lipstick on the guy and he hadn't yet worn it off. Not abnormal for a black cat to have a partial pink lip.

Letting his gaze go unfocused, Stuart noticed the swirling darkness over the cat. This was fog or smoke-like, not the heavier darkness that hung around Courtney. Stuart opened the carrier and placed his hand on Wilbur. The cat's fur felt cool. Digging fingers through the thick, heavy coat, even the skin on the cat felt cooler than it should. The cat breathed deeply, though, which was good. The heat from the lamp reached him.

Stuart looked again at the aura. Nothing seemed attached to the cat. The darkness hovered over him, waiting for an opportunity. Auras didn't normally wait for an opportunity. They weren't sentient. Somehow, this darkness was.

Stuart backed away from the carrier. The cat, of course, was the priority. Without the cat, the bond-mate was useless. He drew in a breath and let it out. They needed to help Wilbur before the darkness figured out how to invade his… Stuart searched for a word. Soul was the closest he could come.

DREW

Drew didn't like the guy from Base Command. Stuart. He looked like an extra on a movie set of a rural town. Drew knew people who dressed like Stuart did, still. The flannel slightly outdated but still service-able. Neat and clean but not fancy. The haircut ordinary.

What bothered him was the guy's face. It was so ordinary as to be completely forgettable. In fact, the moment Drew looked elsewhere he forgot what Stuart looked like. He could sort of remember the hair because it was just a haircut, but if he had to go to the police to describe Stuart, Drew knew he would fail.

He stayed in the room, watching Stuart work with Amber. Stuart held her hand, lightly, at least, so Drew couldn't be angry about that. Amber had seemed relaxed enough after it was over. When they walked over to Wilbur's kennel, Drew moved to the other side of the room.

Stuart looked inside the carrier first, taking a long, measuring look. Then, Amber pulled the blanket out that Drew had put in there. Wilbur laid quietly on the blanket, not even noticing the movement, or not appearing to. Amber drew in some breaths in the way she did before working on someone.

"*How is she doing that without Minnett?*" Drew asked.

"*Stuart serves as a sort of bridge. He can fill in the gaps left without Minnett in the room, though Minnett is monitoring the proceedings.*" Mack's response came quickly and easily.

"*I don't trust him,*" Drew said. He often talked out loud to Mack even when the cat wasn't in the room. Everyone in the clowder was used to hearing people have a one-sided conversation. In the medic room, Drew didn't want to distract Amber. He really didn't want Stuart to know what he was talking about.

"*He's as trustworthy as anyone at Base Command. They do not normally mean us any harm,*" Mack said.

If that wasn't a comment that ached with questions Drew didn't know what was. As if Base Command wasn't at all trustworthy. Normally they do not mean harm.

"*Normally?*" Drew asked. It was all he could get out.

There was a lot of information flowing from Mack to him, more than could be spoken in words. Mack had heard all the questions and his knowledge was all there but it was moving too fast for Drew to catch it consciously. One day he'd wake up knowing this stuff, but not that day.

"*We have heard that there is concern the problem is with this portal. One way to shut off access to another world is to destroy the portal. The problem is that it will destroy anything linked to the portal, which means the clowder. It would also destroy Stuart and possibly much of the surrounding area, though we cannot say for certain as no portal has been closed on this world,*" Mack said.

Drew felt his temper rising. They'd just destroy them to get rid of the problem? "*How long before they decide?*"

"*There is no set time,*" Mack said. "*It has not been decided and it is up to Stuart to determine. If we are fighting in good faith, it will not happen. If we are becoming infiltrated and more of a problem they will. Shutting down a portal is only a stop-gap and could actually increase the problems. After all, if there is no portal anytime a world brushes ours creatures just appear, anywhere."*

But they were only one portal.

Drew left the room. He didn't want Stuart to turn and perhaps realize how frustrated he was. He didn't know what the powers of a watcher at Base Command were but the watchers, in general, had a good sense of people around them. They weren't easy to sneak up on.

Although it was mid-afternoon, the basement lights were on around the great room. No light filtered in through the closed shutters. The light fixture on the ceiling was a large stained glass dome that had cats on it. Both a pool room kind of look and a cat lover's dream. It fit the house. The brighter lamp in the corner was off.

The downside of the shutters was that you couldn't tell if it was snowing.

"It has just started again," Mack said. *"Wheelie has gone up to his window as a lookout. There are several windows on the third floor where there are no shutters."*

At least Drew hadn't been sent upstairs to watch the sky.

"Fin is near the front door. They have added boards across it from the garage along with locking down the garage further," Mack said. *"Cari is in the breakfast nook guarding the door into the house from the garage. Someone will be on watch at all times, lest the people outside break in."*

Kayley sat watching Chase's room. The door was closed.

"How is he?" Drew asked, walking towards Kayley. He didn't like the feel of the air as he got closer to the door. It felt the way the air did before he was about to fight.

"He's in there and not making much noise," Kayley said. "I think he's asleep. But he's not himself at all."

"Do you feel the tension?" Drew asked. "I feel like I'm on guard here."

Kayley cocked her head. Then she indicated no. As she shook her head, she changed her mind. "There is something. It's just, I think it's grown and I've been here a bit and gotten used to it. It feels subtle to me unless I focus on it."

"I don't like it," Drew said.

"*I have let Minnett know*," Mack said. "*Amber and Stuart will investigate this as soon as they have worked on Wilbur and Matt.*"

"Not sure there's anything much to like about what's happening. Riley has been holed up in the library trying to find anything in the frost witch legends to help but all she's getting are how they take over and destroy worlds. If you talk to her very long about what she knows, you feel like you should just give up and wait to die," Kayley said. She tapped on the tablet she'd been reading on.

"I wonder how long it takes," Drew said, "when they destroy a world. I mean, is it a week. A month? Decades? They eat life energy, from what I understand. How long does it take to destroy all life?"

Kayley swung her leg and shook her head. "Interesting question. Because however long it takes, it tells us how long we have to find an answer.

Drew looked around the darkened room. Something banged on the door upstairs, the extra boards and shutters causing the house to shake and thunder. No matter how long they had, he wasn't sure it would be nearly long enough.

CHASE

Chase wandered through dreams. He knew they were dreams. Birds rarely flew so close to him when he wasn't concentrating on hiding. They were so near he could see each of the orange feathers on the breast. He noted how the feathers gave way to more orange feathers with scallops of palest white between them. Brown back feathers crowded up to the brighter orange, white lines appearing here and there.

The bright yellow beak caught his eye while the robin watched from eyes so deep brown they looked almost black. The bird was so close, Chase could see the difference between the deep brown and the black pupil.

The bird decided it didn't like Chase's scrutiny and flew off. Chase walked behind it, following. Robins were typically only harbingers of spring. The chill around him told Chase it wasn't spring in his dream. It was fall, maybe winter.

The grass was still bright green, particularly where it edged up against cream concrete. Chase knew the concrete. He was in the park—his park. Ahead, in the direction the bird flew were the trees where the portal waited.

Chase floated along. In a dream, it wasn't fair to walk. He floated, noting the individual blades of grass and how some grew longer than others, some fatter, crowding out their thinner cousins. In other places, the grass hardly grew at all, the creamy gray of a dull patch nearly hidden beneath the healthier shoots.

The details would have impressed even Trag, but Chase didn't hear him.

The robin disappeared. Chase settled in next to his favorite tree. Daylight began to fade, the colors going from gold and blue to pink and blue. A shadow waited nearby. Trag. Chase heard the sounds of cars heading down the street, workers coming home from their jobs. A car honked, particularly loud.

Trag flicked an ear.

"Humans have so little patience," Trag commented in Chase's mind.

Joy flooded Chase when he heard the voice, the low scratchy sound that made him think of old records that had seen too much use. His body shook with the joy, so large he couldn't contain it.

"Chill," Trag said.

The voice wasn't quite as scratchy. It was like a recording of his cat's voice entering his dream.

Chase waited by the tree, getting comfortable against the scratchy bark. The day smelled of dampness. A hint of autumn hung in the air in the slight nip of the temperature and in the scent of something beginning to rot.

It crept up on him quickly, becoming strong, like something had died and a breeze was bringing the rotting smell to him. Except there wasn't much of a breeze.

Trag was lolling around, half-asleep as if he didn't even notice. The cat should have been alert.

"Do you smell that?" Chase asked.

"*Odd*," Trag said. His real voice, the voice that spoke in Chase's head all the time. Or had until recently.

Something was wrong. Chase felt it. He wanted to run from the wood and the portal. He ought to have Trag contact the other cats.

Instead, he felt the tingle along his spine that said the portal was opening. This tingle was different from nerves. It went deeper, like an itch he couldn't reach to scratch. It stopped almost as soon as it started. Whatever had come through was small.

Chase sat up alert.

"*You got it?*" he asked Trag.

No response from the cat. Trag snoozed nearby, completely oblivious to anything.

Chase stood up. In front of him was a shimmer of pale blue light that reminded him of ice. The light began to take a shape, becoming an ice sculpture rather than a light. The woman it formed appeared to come from his own mind. Her figure was Courtney's but taller, slightly more rounded. The face might have been Courtney's in a perfect world.

Color flowed into the ice and the not-Courtney stood before him, her cheeks too pink, her eyes far too wise. She looked him up and down, like a farmer judging a steer.

Chase didn't move.

"You are Chase Anders, watcher for this portal," Not-Courtney said. Her voice was kind of hollow, just a little off like something had listened to a recording of Courtney's voice and not gotten it exactly right. Like Trag's voice from moments ago.

Chase felt ill, his stomach twisting and rising. Bile rose.

Not-Courtney waved a hand at him and he felt nothing at all.

"Take me with you, little man. Let me learn your world," Not-Courtney said.

Chase backed up a step.

Not-Courtney reached out her hands. She was naked. Her breasts tipped upwards as if longing for him. Terrified though he was, Chase wanted to reach for her, wanted to touch those breasts which were more perfect than the real Courtney's.

He tried to back up again but a tree blocked his path. His body lusted for Not-Courtney. He felt it in every cell, that sense that he'd die if he didn't touch her, the agony of waiting and wanting. His mind told him he shouldn't touch her.

Not-Courtney moved forward, her hands reaching out to grasp his. Chase let her place his hand on her breast, felt the slight movement beneath his fingers. He groaned.

Then he was hugging her, wanting to kiss, to hold her, to make love to her there in the park, uncaring of who might be around. The fact that Trag wasn't speaking to him didn't even factor into Chase's mind, he was so caught up in the desire.

Instead of lips reaching hers, Chase was left with only traces of icy water on his hands. He looked down. Nothing was there.

Confused he fell back onto his butt. He leaned against the tree, closing his eyes. Whatever had happened made him tired.

Moments later, Trag was waking him in the woods.

"*Fall asleep?*" Trag teased. As if he hadn't.

"*I guess?*" Chase said. He wasn't sure how he could have but he didn't remember what happened. He remembered the smell, which was gone.

"*Fortunately, I stayed awake,*" Trag snickered.

"*How long was I out?*" Chase asked. It didn't feel right. The sun was in the wrong place, the sky more pink and gray than pink and blue.

Trag paused. "*I'm not certain,*" he said.

"I won't tell if you won't," Chase laughed. It wasn't good to fall asleep in front of the portal. However, he was connected enough that he'd know when the portal opened. His eyes would open and he'd be ready. Nothing could have gotten through while he slept.

Chase was certain of it. Mostly.

The feeling stayed with him for the rest of the night.

A loud thundering woke Chase, really woke him that time. He sat up in his bed, the covers falling around him. His chest felt heavy and tight. Something had come through the portal that evening. While he was on duty. It hadn't come last night. It had come a week ago.

He ought to tell someone.

The room was too cold, though. Besides, Chase thought the clowder might do something to him. He didn't know what, but he was certain it was bad. The itchy sensation of a portal opening ran up his spine again, though this time it felt bigger, like it was closer to him. Stomach rolling, Chase curled up again, hoping he didn't puke in his bed.

As soon as he curled on his side, Chase's body relaxed. It probably didn't matter what had happened. Not really.

STUART

Stuart breathed out, trying to process the things he'd seen in Matt's energetic body. There was something alive there, something sentient. He knew it deep down. The smell of rot reached his nose but it didn't come from any of the people in the room. It came from the room itself, something outside the humans. Whatever had reached those people was in the air.

What he really wanted was a quiet place to process, to send his information back to Base Command, and then do his own thinking and make connections. What he needed to do was help Amber work on Wilbur. The cat was the priority.

"We need to work on healing Wilbur. Is Minnett up to helping you or can you work with me if Minnett watches through your eyes?" Stuart asked.

Amber's eyes widened as if the idea hadn't even occurred to her. She looked around the treatment room at Courtney, who had her eyes closed, her breathing even like she was sleeping. Stuart knew she was faking sleep, or something was. The darkness in her energetic body suggested that perhaps the real Courtney was asleep and whatever was inside her was watching. It was active enough that Stuart was aware of it behind him, making his shoulders twitch in anticipation.

Matt, on the other hand, had his eyes closed but his breathing didn't suggest sleep. Rather it suggested he was struggling to consciousness. Whatever he had to say was likely to be interesting. Stuart looked forward to the conversation.

Amber frowned and moved over to the carrier. "I think it would be easier if we moved Wilbur over to the table," she said. She started lifting the towel that held the cat, but Stuart took over. It was only a few steps to the table furthest from the door. After he laid Wilbur down, leaving a hand on him, Amber raised the bed to the level of her waist.

Wilbur didn't seem to notice. Amber brought the heat lap over to the cat and made sure it remained on him, warming him. It was higher up than before, but Stuart and Amber would need hands near the cat, especially Amber.

She bit her lip slightly. "I might need items. The black things looked like parasites of a sort, so maybe glass jars with a lid?"

Stuart nodded. "Where?"

Amber pointed towards the wall of cabinets which wasn't particularly helpful. Stuart found the jars on the second try. They were all empty clear glass jars with lids. They might have held herbs at one point based on the smells in the cupboard. Cinnamon, ginger, clove, and turmeric, though Stuart knew that Amber didn't know them by those names.

He brought two jars over to the table. "Anything else?"

"I can't think of anything," Amber said. "But most things are in the cupboards. If I need to stop to find something that's not there, we can."

Something pounded on the shutters upstairs. The insulation in the medic room was good because the sound was fainter than he would have expected. Stuart didn't think anything could get in easily. For now, they needed to concentrate on Wilbur. He nodded at Amber who had also heard the noise. She drew in a breath, readying herself.

Stuart hoped they didn't have to stop. Amber took his hand. He steadied himself on the floor, planting his feet a bit wider. He drew in energy and let it flow to Amber. Her eyes were already closed and when he closed his, they were already deep into Wilbur's energetic body.

There weren't parasites there. Only shadows. Amber was having trouble gathering those up. Stuart imagined a vacuum cleaner, one of the tall fancy upright ones in purple, and handed that over to her.

He felt her chuckle. But it worked. The vacuum nozzle pulled in the smoke and gathered it in the energetic bag. Stuart heard the slight hum of the machine as Amber used it. He hadn't realized that he had given it so much power. Maybe it was Amber and Minnett's abilities that augmented his own, nicely. Whatever the reason, they could use all the advantages they could get.

Once the smoky cloud was gone, Amber handed him the vacuum. Stuart opened his eyes and placed the energy into a glass jar and closed the lid. They'd find a way to dispose of it later, even if it meant sending it out to the dead area on the other side of the portal.

Closing his eyes again, Stuart watched as Amber dug more closely through Wilbur's energetic body. The cat appeared clear. No parasites hanging around. Only the dark cloud that had seemed to want to get into his field but was unable to. Base Command would want to know that the cats were slightly immune to the influences.

As Amber came out, she shook her head. "Minnett and I didn't see anything. I think he's pretty clear."

"Now for Matt," Stuart said. Amber looked a bit pale, but she ought to be able to work on Matt. Or at least start.

Amber moved Wilbur to the floor. It was probably a good idea if the cat was really that sound asleep. Stuart didn't expect Wilbur would roll off the table, but you never knew. Better safe than sorry. Shahanna the tortoiseshell cat with the pretty orange toes came in and snuggled against Wilbur.

"Did they want to snuggle earlier?" Stuart asked, following Amber to Matt, holding a couple of empty jars.

"No," Amber said. "They didn't know what was going on earlier. Anastasia was concerned that he might have been carrying something that would harm the rest of them. Minnett told them what happened to her with Courtney and we had no way of knowing if a cat cuddling up to Wilbur might get the same energetic treatment."

"I thought that Minnett was injured when she was healing Courtney, connected to her energetic body," Stuart said.

"We were," Amber said, the "we" a subtle reminder that she'd been injured too. "But we don't know if you need that level of close contact, particularly when the cats are already connected telepathically."

Stuart filed away the abundance of caution. At this point it was smart. Later, it could be a liability, though as they learned more, perhaps they would be less cautious.

Amber stood over Matt. Stuart reached out his hand. They flowed into Matt's energetic body as they had earlier. Stuart created another vacuum for her to vacuum up the shadowy iciness that lingered around Matt's organs.

She returned the vacuum to him. Stuart placed the energetic vacuum cleaner bag in a jar. It was possible that the magic that made the construct appear in Amber's mind was strong enough to hold the darkness, but he wished to take no chances. He, too, was cautious.

Letting himself flow back into Matt's body. Stuart noted

Amber had created tweezers for her hands. She carefully plucked each of the small hair-like creatures from Matt's spine. It was slow and tedious work. The fact that Amber kept at it long after Stuart was ready to take a break impressed him.

Stuart's energy was faltering by the time she reached the mid-spine where the last of the tendrils were. Amber did one final pass to be sure she hadn't missed any. Stuart didn't notice anything. He closed the lid of the jar and they returned to the room.

Amber opened her eyes and then slumped backward. It was all Stuart could do to catch her before she hit the floor.

COURTNEY

Courtney's back ached. She felt cold. The heat lamp was over the table next to her and hadn't been moved when the cat was moved. The room smelled of feline musk and a light acid scent. It smelled more of sickness than cleansers.

She kept her eyes closed and tried to adjust her body so that it didn't hurt so much. How could sitting on a table hurt that badly? The upper part of the table was raised a bit so she could drink. She was still thirsty, but not parched. If someone offered her more water, she'd drink but she worried about the bathroom thing.

The weird man with the ordinary face was still in the room along with Amber. They'd healed the cat and were working on the guy on the table who wasn't Chase. Courtney tried to pull at the restraints but nothing was happening. Even so, she couldn't help trying.

Amber and that man talked about healing. She'd seen darkness coming off the cat. Some of it had wafted over to her. Watching them work on the guy, she thought she saw faces in shadows laughing at her. One appeared beneath the arm of the man on the table, peering out like it might have been in the fold of a shirt or other optical illusion. Another appeared over the group and looked down, laughing.

Courtney wasn't certain if the faces were laughing at her or at Amber and the weird guy.

She wanted to say something, but couldn't quite get the words out. Besides, if she spoke up, they might discover she was crazy and needed help. Or maybe they'd know their experiments were working.

So she laid there, the aches in her low back growing. Courtney got cold. The room hadn't felt cold to her, but the longer Amber worked, the colder the room got. It wasn't Courtney's imagination. She could see her breath, an icy fog coming from her mouth each time she exhaled.

Shivering, Courtney tried to curl up around her body to preserve her warmth but she had no way to do so. She closed her eyes, trying to ignore her discomfort.

It didn't help.

With her eyes closed, she imagined finding heat. Amber and the weird guy were standing not far from her. She felt their body heat. Courtney imagined feeling it more. She started to feel warmer. That was a good thing.

It stopped as soon as her focus stopped. The furnace clicked on. The hum sounded like laughter. Courtney continued to shiver, feeling the chill deep in her bones. She kept pulling the body heat to her. It would warm her a little but dissipate just as quickly.

The laugher she heard got louder.

Amber fell backward, almost into Courtney's table. The weird guy caught her and lowered her down.

Courtney wondered if she had anything to do with Amber's falling. She couldn't have, though, because she didn't do anything.

"So cold," Courtney whispered, not certain that the weird

guy heard. He was busy carrying Amber towards the far door. So much for her room being a clinic room. It was probably the evil experimenting room.

Courtney closed her eyes, trying to ignore her discomfort. The room seemed to be warmer now that they weren't standing next to her. It was almost as if their very presence had brought the cold.

The shivers slowed and Courtney tried to ease into the greater level of comfort. Her back was still aching. The angle of the bed was wrong. She wanted it further up or lower down. She wanted to pull her knees up to her chest or move her hips. However long she'd been in that one position was too long. This was bordering on cruel.

Laughter bubbled up but didn't make it out of her mouth as Courtney realized she thought that an evil medical experimentation place wouldn't be cruel. She wasn't thinking clearly.

She longed for the dreams of her little house where she might climb into her bed and go to sleep and feel or see nothing. Even if she had to be cold, her little house drew her. Never mind that she'd be alone there. Courtney wanted to be anywhere but in that room.

She ought to be scared but she wasn't, not any longer. That disappeared somewhere along the line. Now she was getting angry and frustrated. The anger warmed her, which was always good. Unfortunately, no matter what, she remained powerless, waiting to be rescued.

"You've got to go out on your own," her dad had told her when she wanted a condo. "It's like you think living there will be like living in a dorm where there's always someone to rescue you."

"I've lived in an apartment for years," Courtney had protested. No one rescued her. She just listened to other people moving around inside their own worlds, taking comfort in the fact that people were there. If things went bad she could race outside and scream.

Her dad had shaken his head. "Living in the real world means living on your own. If you aren't going to get married, you need to be able to take care of yourself."

"Hello? Apartment? Years?" Courtney had said, getting mad.

"An apartment doesn't force you to take care of the exterior. You just call maintenance when something goes wrong. How often did you ask for a plumber?"

Courtney's apartment kitchen sink backed up at least once a month. She called every few months. It wasn't her fault the sink backed up. It had been a problem since day one. Her dad seemed to think her inability to fix it was a problem. That she relied on others too much.

He said she was dependent. She worked at her own job. She was out on her own.

"You need a real job that uses your degree." Again her dad completely misunderstood her life.

"I do insurance billing for a medical clinic. It pays better than a bookkeeping job. I didn't pass the CPA exam but I'll take it again," Courtney said. Maybe. Maybe she was lying. She'd only studied for it because one of her classmates was studying. However, it had been disheartening to not pass, though many didn't.

"Is there any upward mobility?" her dad had asked.

"Clinic manager," Courtney had said.

"Glorified secretary," her dad had answered.

Courtney was always going to be dependent if no one recognized what she could do. The wallowing in her frustrations with her father warmed her. Courtney realized she was less uncomfortable than she had been.

Maybe she could keep doing that.

Amber and the other guy were gone. Courtney thought

the cat was still in the room, behind her head. The guy on the table still seemed out.

Courtney closed her eyes and reached out to try and feel his warmth. She touched it but it was weak. Something told her not to take too much. Like she could just take energy. How cool was that? That was a power her father would never understand. Courtney smiled, thinking of taking all of her father's energy, watching him wither and shrink into cold nothingness.

She felt more awake and aware as she did so, listening to the sounds around her. The guy on the table snored softly, resting easier. She heard the cat behind her shift position, a sound so subtle she was surprised she noticed, but all her senses seemed enhanced.

The sound of pounding outside reached her ears. It had been going on for some time off and on but it wasn't particularly noticeable in the room. Now it sounded louder like her ears were better.

Yet another weird thing happening to her body. Courtney closed her eyes and tried to rest, wondering where everyone was.

Drew hurried upstairs. Someone—something?—was really banging on the door up there. Although the sounds had intrigued Kayley as well, she stayed in the basement, keeping an eye on those covered entrances as well as watching over Chase's room.

Fin was at the front door along with Anson and Julia. They were looking at the windows.

"Axel says there are ten people out there banging on the shutters and the door," Mack said. *"It appears they're testing how easily the shutters move and what happens when they bang on them. Wheelie and Axel have bets on whether the people go around back to pound on the shutters there or if they continue to work on the door."*

Mack was downstairs with Boyd and Chara cuddling with Minnett. Amber and Stuart were working on Wilbur. Drew felt torn between going down to assist the two of them or staying upstairs in case of a fight. He was always an extra, maybe needed, maybe not.

The outside group banged on the door, again. Upstairs the sound made Drew's whole body quake, not in fear but from the thuds moving the house.

Fin brought over a chair and stood on it so he could look out the moon-shaped window over the door.

"Three people hitting the door," Fin said, ducking down.

"Four are moving around the house. The rest must be on the porch where neither Fin nor Wheelie can see them," Mack said.

Drew wasn't surprised when something banged on the shutters on the backdoor. Looking over that way, he saw Tom in the great room, backing up a bit, probably so he had room to move if needed.

"The group around back is testing windows all around the house," Mack said moments later.

More banging from both sides of the house.

"This is ridiculous," Julia said. "We could go out and rush them."

"Not a good idea," Mack said. *"It's snowing pretty hard. They could be doing this to try and draw people out so that they're pushed into the snowfall."*

"Think they're trying to lure us out?" Fin asked, no doubt having heard Chara telling him what Mack had told Drew.

"There's intelligence to this attack," Anson said. He was standing near the furthest end of the front room, angled as if he might see out through the shutters. "Everything Riley's found suggests that if we are facing frost witches, they're smart. They use hallucinations on people so that they willingly give up their life force. The people outside were probably tricked into coming here to try and get us out in the snow."

"Matt wasn't used like that," Drew said. He frowned. What was different about Matt?

"Maybe they couldn't quite get to him in time," Julia said. "Maybe it takes longer for us. They got to Chase."

And Chase was downstairs in his room, guarded only by Kayley.

"What's going on downstairs?" Drew asked Mack.

"Amber and Stuart are in the medic room. They have worked on Wilbur and he is doing better. Shahanna is with him. They are starting work on Matt."

"What about Chase?"

"He is in his room," Mack said.

"Could he work with someone to open the hurricane shutters in his room so he can get out?" Drew asked. He spoke out loud in case Mack didn't have the information he needed.

Mack's response was a general he didn't know because he didn't know much about hurricane shutters.

"It's not impossible," Julia said. "I put the lock on his window outside, but any lock is breakable. Chase would just have to raise the window."

"And stay quiet," Anson said. He was already at the stairs. Tom followed. Drew went after them. Julia stayed upstairs with Fin. Someone had to watch those windows. They couldn't all go running in every direction each time something happened.

By the time Drew reached the bottom of the basement stairs, Anson and Tom had moved Kayley's chair out of the way and had opened Chase's door. The room was brighter than it should have been.

Drew hurried over.

Chase's room wasn't that big. With Chase near the window, the hurricane shutters open, and Anson and Tom pulling him back, the room was well over capacity. Kayley was trying to climb onto Chase's desk to get to the glass and close it. If Drew wanted to go further in, he'd have to climb on Chase's bed.

A group of four people stood outside Chase's room. To Drew's eyes, they looked like a family in pajamas and sweats. A bigger man was holding a little boy on his shoulders so the boy could pull the screen off. The window was already open.

Kayley finished crawling over the desk and started to close it. The screen was far enough off that another child put a tiny toy car on the ledge so the window couldn't latch.

Drew didn't think Kayley saw the car.

He jogged into the big basement room with the pool table. The shutters in that room were still closed leaving the place in gray dimness even with the lights.

He grabbed a pool cue, the longest one there, which when placed on the floor rose up to his chest. Hopefully, that would be long enough.

Drew turned and jogged back to the room, holding the rounded cue like he was a martial artist using a bo-stick. Not his thing, but he'd watched Fin work out often enough.

Drew could fake it.

He got back to the room. Chase was still struggling with Tom and Anson. They were grunting at each other as elbows found the soft tissue of an abdomen or a low back. A swear as someone got hit across the face.

Drew kept to the wall and worked his way towards Kayley. She'd noticed the car and tried to push it out, but a woman, perhaps the mom, had grabbed Kayley's arm and was trying to pull her out.

Drew set the stick down and grabbed Kayley around the waist and pulled. The mom might have been strong enough to pull Kayley off balance and get her arm outside—had snow hit it? Did that matter?—but Drew was far stronger.

The mom dropped her grip on Kayley's arm when she began to be pulled inside.

Drew pushed his way to the window, knocking Anson into Chase, which knocked Chase onto the bed.

Drew pulled the window down.

Fingers and hands blocked his way. Kayley used the pool cue to slap at them until they let go. Drew closed the window and locked it.

"We need a board to nail up in here," Kayley said.

"Riley's going to fetch one," Mack said.

Drew knew they'd hear about that. Riley did not like having to get involved in physical things. However, it wasn't like there were huge swaths of information on the Frost Witches in their library or on the internet. She couldn't be that busy.

No doubt the cats had conveyed approximately how big the board needed to be. Hopefully, Riley wouldn't be pushing anything too big down the stairs.

"I'll go help," Kayley said. "Watch this window and listen outside for me, okay?"

Drew nodded. He ought to be the one going up, but Kayley would be faster. Besides, no one was pulling him out a window. At least his size made him useful.

STUART

Stuart struggled more than he should trying to get Amber to the office. It wasn't far, only a few feet, across an odd little alcove. Maybe he ought to have placed her on the table behind them, but he didn't think he could lift her.

The office had carpeting, though as he knelt lowering her to the ground, it felt colder on his knees than it should have. People were running down the stairs. Someone groaned. Maybe it was him or perhaps Amber.

All Stuart knew was that he was far more fatigued than he expected to be.

Closing his eyes, he inspected his energetic body. Normally, he saw his organs in bright colors, bright yellow for his stomach, rich, deep green for the liver, midnight blue for the kidneys, ruby for his heart. When he looked now, everything was pale. The yellow a pale color like urine after flooding the body with water. The green was so light it was barely there.

Stuart drew in some energy from around him. The ground beneath the house was dying but not as dead as the area around the park. Something else was pulling energy. Not just from the land but from the living things around it. The energy and magic of the earth should have been enough even if every single one of the billions of people on earth suddenly decided to connect and draw energy.

A human could only hold so much.

Whatever was drawing the energy was taking so much it wasn't just drawing from the land but killing the creatures that made the land their home. Another thing to mention to Base Command.

Stuart felt in his pockets for his phone. He found it. Pulled it out, resting his arm.

He needed food. He pushed himself up, re-pocketing the phone. Amber probably needed food and something to drink.

The stairs seemed impossibly long. He took a moment to curse a clowder house that didn't have an elevator. That should have been required. After all, didn't the US have an ADA requirement? The clowders ought to comply even if they weren't a real business.

He climbed slowly and made it to the upper floor just as something banged on the front door. He'd been vaguely aware of the banging earlier. It was louder up there.

A couple of women came out carrying a large piece of plywood and moved around him. The older of the two looked at him. Riley.

"Do you need help?" she asked him.

"I need some food," Stuart said. "So does Amber. I think the last healing took a lot of energy out of us."

"I got this," the younger woman called over her shoulder. Kayley, if Stuart, didn't miss his guess. His brain felt slow and sluggish like he was still half-asleep.

"Thanks," Riley told Kayley.

Then, Riley moved slowly, painfully to the kitchen. This

was her best and it wasn't much better than Stuart at his worst. It made him sad. Even as a researcher she ought to be in less pain.

Stuart unconsciously reached out, only to drop his hand realizing he was too depleted to give her even his minimal help. A good healer at Base Command would have made Riley feel ten years younger. He would have given her a bit of relief, but now, he didn't think he could do that without hurting himself.

Riley pulled out some juice and poured him a glass.

"We need to make a tray for Amber," Stuart said. He slugged back the juice feeling the coolness in his throat and the sugar reaching his stomach, soon to be transported easily to his cells.

Riley turned and reached for another glass from the white cabinetry. She poured more orange juice. She pulled out some cheese and gave it to Stuart.

"Anastasia says Amber is sleeping on the floor of her office," Riley said. It was like a question but not a question.

"Something wiped us out while working on Matt," Stuart said. "He's clear, now, at least for the moment."

Riley went to the cupboard and got out a can of soup that you could microwave and drink. It smelled good. The cheese was nice but not as good as the soup smelled.

Stuart wandered around to the other side of the big island and found bread to make a sandwich. Riley gave him fixings without being asked, chopping up some lettuce and onion in case he wanted that.

The more he ate, the hungrier he got. Stuart piled everything on. Dark rye bread, bakery made. Nicer than he'd have purchased for himself. Thick sliced turkey. Havarti cheese and cheddar cheese. Lettuce, onion, mayo, and mustard.

It took longer to make than to eat. The soup was done. Riley carried both the glasses out of the kitchen.

"I'll be back up to fix Amber more food, unless you want to. Anything in the fridge is fine."

Stuart opened the doors, looking around at what might be good. In the freezer, he found breakfast sandwiches. He used the microwave to make two of those. He ate one. Saved one for Amber.

He searched the pantry. Came up with a large chocolate bar, the fancy kind of dark chocolate that was supposed to have health properties. He broke off a bit of that and ate it. He pulled out a different flavor for Amber. He grabbed cheese as well and headed down to help Riley feed her.

Hopefully, once they got the orange juice in her, she'd be more awake.

Once at the bottom of the stairs, Stuart was awake and aware enough to notice that several people were pounding a board across Chase's window. Something had happened. Chase was trying to get out or people were trying to get in using his window.

Things were happening fast. Stuart hadn't expected things to happen so fast. He set the breakfast sandwich down on the desk for Amber. He pulled out his phone and sat behind her desk.

Riley was holding Amber's body up, helping her sip at the orange juice. A little of it dribbled down her chin, but she seemed to be drinking it pretty well.

Stuart dialed Darla.

"What?"

He summarized what he knew. He placed the chocolate on the desk, noting how tidily kept the surface was. The books on the shelves behind him were a little messy. Mostly thick acupuncture books that weighed perhaps five or ten pounds each and a few medical tomes. In between were thinner paperbacks that promised specialty information.

Riley reached up for the soup mug. He watched Amber's

head raise further up, mostly on her own, though Riley supported her. Amber's hands gripped the mug, her knuckles almost white. At least she'd soon be able to eat on her own.

Riley grabbed the breakfast sandwich and offered it to Amber. The paper towel it was wrapped in was returned to the desk in seconds. Barely enough time to have taken one large bite. He had to admit he knew the feeling and Amber seemed to have felt it even more than he did.

"You were drained?" Darla repeated.

"And the healer," Stuart said, earning him a glare from Riley. Maybe he should have used a name. Darla wouldn't have cared. She'd have known who he meant.

"By healing?"

"Or by something that happened while we were healing Matt."

"Keep an eye on this," Darla ordered. As if he was too stupid to recognize that that might be something to watch.

"Of course," Stuart said, as mildly as possible. It probably didn't matter. Darla was beyond the ability to note such subtleties.

The dial tone told him she had hung up, probably completely unaware of his thoughts.

"I've never been so wiped out after a healing," Amber said.

"I believe something sapped our energies while we were in there," Stuart said.

"Matt?" Amber asked. There was a pause in the chewing.

"I didn't get that impression. I didn't see any energy being sapped and that would be something I would notice. I was a watcher. I might not know healing and the body quite like you do, but I was trained to see incursions, wherever they occur."

Amber mumbled something. She pushed herself up, though she wobbled a bit. Riley held out a hand.

"I need more food," Amber said.

"Let's go back up," Stuart agreed. He pushed himself up. The food was beginning to make a difference. He didn't normally eat much so he'd have to slow himself down lest he make himself sick.

Amber let Riley walk her out the door. They all walked slowly up the stairs. Stuart wanted to know more about what was going on with Chase, but his place was with Amber for the moment.

"If it wasn't Matt, how was our energy sapped?" Amber asked.

"My best guess would be Courtney," Stuart said. "If I'm right, we ought to remove Wilbur and Matt from the medic room. If Matt can be isolated in his room, we can scan him again before we let him wander freely."

Amber nodded. Stuart heard people moving quickly down in the basement. He had no doubt the cats would have passed his orders on.

"For now, I think we eat and drink and maybe get a nap," Stuart said. The long sofa in the great room called him. He'd bunk there for the moment and snooze. Later, he'd find an unoccupied room.

"I don't think I've ever been this hungry in my life," Amber said.

"It's your body's way of trying to get you back on track energetically," Stuart said.

Amber nodded. Stuart wanted to say more but bit back another response. Amber knew this, probably better than most of their healers. She didn't need him preaching to her like she was an infant.

CHASE

Chase felt arms around him, pulling him towards the bed. He didn't remember getting up. The last thing he remembered was dreaming, or remembering that day in the park. He thought he woke after that before returning to sleep, dreamless.

The room was colder than it should have been. The sounds of scratching at the screen and a few grunts reached him. The pale cream of the walls and the darker wood of his dresser reached his eyes. The sheen of the tile in the bathroom drew him but he couldn't get a handle on anything.

Chase stopped moving his body, letting those that had grabbed him bring him towards the bed. The grunting seemed quieter. A squeal of the window being lowered sounded. The chill draft cut off.

"What's…?" Chase asked. He reached out for Trag, hoping the cat could explain. No one else was hurrying to tell him.

"You were going to let people inside," Trag said. There was no explanation for why he could hear the cat. Chase didn't care why suddenly. Only that he could hear him. He felt whole again.

Chase wanted to crawl up the telepathic link and hug Trag. He'd been so alone. He wanted to be closer to the cat. He reached out, hoping to hear more about what happened, to see it through Trag's eyes.

The hairs on the back of his neck raised. Something was there with him. And it wasn't Trag.

"Trag?" Chase asked, pausing in his search for the cat's memories and mind.

"You've been acting oddly," the cat said evenly. There was a hint of censure in his voice, but not anger.

"Something's here with us," Chase thought.

Trag was silent. Chase felt him looking, searching. Sorrow. Then like a door slamming shut, Chase was alone.

Anger reached him, hot anger, filling him, burning him from the inside.

Chase doubled over in pain. He was being pushed over onto the bed. He brought his knees up to crawl, trying to protect his stomach. Someone touched his side, just barely brushing him, yet pain flared.

He groaned though he didn't mean to. He had to tell them.

Chase opened his mouth but nothing came out. His throat burned hot. His lips chapping even as he noted the heat. His eyes itched. He closed them, hoping to the sensation would stop.

Whoever was helping him to the bed, moved away. He felt their body heat moving away. Air circulated around his body, cooling him on the outside, leaving the heat inside his chest and abdomen. Even his hands felt hot. He wanted to look at them, to see if they were red.

People were talking but he was in too much pain to hear them.

"Stop fighting," a voice said. *"It will be easier on you."*

The voice was like Trag trying to imitate Courtney. There

were flashes of words or intonation that sounded like her but it was a voice like Trag's in his head. Chase didn't recognize it.

"Stop fighting."

Chase wasn't aware that he was fighting. He didn't even know that he was supposed to be fighting. He'd been half asleep, hallucinating, trying to exist in his world, and not exactly doing a great job of it. Yet this voice in his head seemed to think he was fighting.

If he could have laughed, Chase would have. His throat and mouth were too hot and dry for anything but a croak to come out.

"Water?" he whispered. Not quite the croak that he worried it would be.

Someone left the room. Hopefully, they'd bring him water. Chase was so thirsty. His throat so hot.

Trag had told him to stop fighting before, but this wasn't Trag. Chase had felt the door slamming shut in his mind, from Trag's side. The cat had cut him off, as forcefully as he could. Chase knew it was possible. Some creatures could piggyback on the telepathic link. Chase had tried warning the cat.

Hopefully, he'd said something soon enough. Trag might think he'd responded too slowly to Courtney's suggestion of giving him up, but Chase loved that cat. He wasn't sure he'd ever love any cat or any human that much again. It wasn't just him projecting that Trag got him. Trag actually did.

The cat knew about all of Chase's flaws and didn't care. The cat accepted him, mostly. It didn't mean he didn't point out when Chase was being an ass, like when Chase had tried to think of a way to compromise with Courtney. There was no compromising on leaving Trag behind, but Chase had wanted to. He did love Courtney in his way. And the sex as good. Something Trag couldn't understand, not after being neutered.

Chase was young. He needed that outlet and Courtney suited him. He'd only wanted to find a way to compromise.

Yet, Trag hadn't seen it like that.

Chase hated that they'd been as much at odds as any bond-mates could be before the cut-off.

Tom handed him a glass of water. Chase's hand shook as he took it and lifted it to his mouth. The cool water soothed his parched tongue and lips. It helped his hot throat, though it hurt just a bit to swallow. He felt like he had a fever.

As the heat dissipated from his insides, he began to feel chilled.

"Something is wrong…" Chase started to say. His throat closed up, threatening to keep him from breathing. He tried clearing it, coughing, but everything was stuck.

His mind focused on getting air, he heard Tom say, "We know."

Chase nodded, letting go of the words. The air came back. He drew in several deep breaths.

"*See what I can do?*" the voice said. "*Surrender.*"

Chase didn't want to surrender. His father said he was a weakling, giving up far too soon. He wanted to fight, to be a hero.

Pain hit him in the abdomen every bit as harsh and as sudden as if Tom had put down the glass and punched him. Chase opened his eyes. Tom was near the window, guarding. They'd keep Tom there as long as they could.

"*Go attack him,*" the voice said. "*The pain will stop.*"

Chase counted to ten in his head. Nothing. He repeated it. Closed his eyes, repeating it again. His hands hugged his torso. He couldn't even groan. How could anyone not know he was in such pain?

"*I know,*" the voice said.

The voice was the cause. He couldn't trust it.

The pain stopped suddenly. Chase breathed in, easier. He felt as if he'd just been in a fight. His arms hung awkwardly, sore from hugging his body. His legs weighted twice what they ought. It was an effort to move into a relaxing position.

"*Better?*" A different voice this time. More masculine.

Chase said yes.

"*I got rid of her for now. Go to sleep,*" it said.

Chase didn't need to be told twice. He was so tired, mentally and physically. He felt as if he were being eaten up from the inside. He needed to rest while he could. As Chase dropped into a deeper sleep, he thought he heard laughter.

Courtney worked on getting out of her restraints. Strength flooded her arms, but no matter how strong she was, she couldn't quite break through the damned things. Her arms moved more, though, as if something had stretched and worn.

Maybe there was hope.

Courtney lifted herself up further, leaning on her elbows and examined the restraint. Caramel-colored leather. A heavy-duty silver buckle, like a belt-buckle, but bigger, held the leather around her wrists. Four holes also reinforced with silver metal. The buckle was in the third hole due to her small wrists.

She wiggled her arm a little, not so much as she wanted but she didn't want to knock herself off-balance either. The little spike that went through the hole moved. Not enough but it moved.

Another round of wiggling. The restraints were definitely looser but from the bottom. She couldn't look over the table to see what she was doing. So far she hadn't needed to. She struggled some more, knowing it would only take one arm free to get her out of there.

She smelled a cat, though she didn't see him. Closing her eyes, tensing in case the furry creature leaped on her, Courtney strained her ears. She thought she heard the tiniest thud of footsteps walking across the room.

Breathing in deeply, like she was sleeping, Courtney hoped to fool the cat.

The soft snores from the table next to her went silent. That alerted her more than anything.

The guy next to her was waking up. He wasn't restrained. Courtney held out a moment of hope that he would help her. She imagined him pulling the buckle apart, opening up the restraints. He'd lend an arm so that she could stand up and leave. The image was so powerful that Courtney almost cried when someone entered the room.

She opened her eyes. The big guy.

He moved behind her. She turned her head to watch as he carried the cat out the door into another room. Courtney breathed in and out. The room smelled better. At least to her. Before, she thought she'd smelled something musky and a tiny bit burnt, like dinner was just starting to stick and burn at the bottom of the pan but was not yet ruined. Heaven knew she'd had enough meals like that, and worse.

Courtney started working the restraints again, stopping quickly when two different people came into the room. She watched as they woke the guy on the table next to hers and helped him stand up. He walked out the door, though a woman walked beside him. To Courtney's unpracticed eye, he appeared to feel better than he had when he came in.

She waited for them to come for her. Thumps and bumps came from upstairs, the same anonymous sounds that could have been anything from water in the pipes to someone dancing on the floor above. Having lived in a three-story apartment building on the second floor, Courtney was used to listening to people upstairs. The room she was in was well-insulated against sounds, leaving her with only the faintest sense of what was going on.

Courtney worked at the restraints while she waited for someone to come. The leather seemed even looser than before. She could raise her arm up to her chest now but not close enough to her face to use her teeth. She tried bending her neck to pull the buckle but it was a bit too far.

Not quite there, Courtney laid back against the table. She was tired, like something outside her had drained all the energy she'd gotten earlier. Now she wanted to lie back and sleep. Instead, she kept working her arm.

In moments, or so it seemed, her shoulder began to ache. The ache crept up into her neck. Between that and a light pressure on her bladder, Courtney was miserable.

"Hey!" she called. "Can I use a bathroom?" Maybe they'd help her?

No one came. She didn't believe that there was no one around. They had to be watching her.

She went back to working the darned restraint, getting more and more frustrated. She was so close.

The door opened. Courtney turned her head. Two women entered, both short and heavily built. She didn't know them.

"I need to use the restroom," Courtney said.

No one said anything, but the two women, removed the restraints, ready to take her to the bathroom. Part of Courtney wanted to strike right then, but she did have a need. Maybe there would be a window in the bathroom.

They walked beside her, not helping her, exactly, but offering a hand, and left the medic room. The small hallway just beyond was darker. Turning, they led her into a big room, thick carpeting cushioned Courtney's bare feet. She remembered the feeling from when she's spent a night with Chase.

His room was over to her left. Courtney moved that direction. The others followed. Once into the hall where she'd turn right to go to Chase's room, she was guided to the left. An open door showed a laundry room with two washers and two dryers, each stacked on top of each other. The room was wide enough for more but Courtney didn't get close enough to look in. The door before that one was a powder room.

The two women allowed her in without following, for which Courtney was grateful. Of course, the room was so tiny, the three of them would never have fit. She brushed the white pedestal sink when she dropped her sweat pants.

A light film of sweat lined her body. Courtney wished for a shower. As she sat, staring at the dark blue walls and the beige tiles, she fantasized about knocking the drywall out along the left side of the powder room and falling into Chase's bathroom, which was probably just on the other side. Then she could escape through his window.

She got a rush of energy fantasizing about escape, but when she stood, Courtney swayed. She was tired. Instead of fleeing for her life, she let the two women lead her back to the medical room. If she were going to die there, so be it. She suddenly felt too tired to care.

A quick nap, barely an hour, on the sofa in the great room, refreshed Stuart. He was up and digging in the fridge for more food in no time. A loud banging on the shutters from the front of the house accompanied him as worked. The noise had probably woken him.

After making another sandwich, this one ham and cheese, Stuart peeked into the front room. Tenny was in a chair swinging her legs, looking at a tablet computer. Stuart noted the tension in her body despite her relaxed air. She was ready for anything.

He finished the sandwich quickly and hurried down the stairs. Kayley was in a club chair near Chase's bedroom. Her bond-mate, Elmore, a sleek cat with brown and black stripes running down his sides sat with her. Both of them looked up at Stuart as he paused at the foot of the stairs. They nodded at him in unison. No doubt Elmore was using his superior hearing to make sure Chase was in the room and not trying to escape, again.

Trag raised his head. He was sleeping alone on a club

chair. Stuart frowned and looked over at Kayley, a question forming.

"You and Amber were resting," Kayley said. "Chase thought something was following him through his bond. Trag cut it off."

None of the other cats were comforting Trag. As sad as it was to see him on the chair, alone, a black shadow of a cat curled tightly around himself, eyes looking tormented, the danger of something having come through was too great. Stuart would check the cat with Amber soon enough.

He turned and went down the hall to his right. Matt's room was at the far corner. It was Stuart's understanding that Anson had the middle room.

Stuart paused before the closed door, uncertain what to do. As Base Command's representative, he could enter anywhere in the house. As a human, though that might be stretching his connection to his species a bit, he didn't wish to invade privacy.

Finally, Stuart raised a hand and knocked. He heard someone moving and soon enough Matt stood in front of him smelling of fresh soap. His hair had a slight curl in it now that it had some life again.

"I was just checking," Stuart said.

"Wilbur and I are fine," Matt said. Stuart peered around the door frame. The bed was centered in the room and Wilbur was near the pillow on the side where the blankets weren't messed up. A small lap fleece in blues and grays was curled up around him. So was a big black cat that Stuart sensed was Anson's bond-mate Navy.

Navy looked up, Wilbur didn't. Yet Stuart got the impression that Wilbur was stronger than he'd been before.

"Fine?" Stuart asked.

"Sleepy. At least Wilbur is. I think he protected me," Matt said.

Stuart slipped into the room, letting his eyes go slightly unfocused. Wilbur was there, the energy around him a clean green and blue. No shadows or smoke swirled with them. Mentally checking the cat let Stuart know that while he was improving, he was not yet at full strength.

"What happened?" Stuart asked Matt. He needed a human version of what went on in the park.

Matt moved around him and sat on the bed. He might look better but he was still not himself. Dressed in Cincinnati Reds pajama bottoms and a green t-shirt with a jaguar on it, Matt looked like a teenager having to tell his dad why he missed curfew.

Stuart tried not to look too intimidating. Matt hadn't done anything wrong, though not contacting the clowder when something came through was a violation. The assumption by everyone was that Wilbur and Matt had been cut off.

"It was weird. I remember it starting to snow. I thought I saw something out there, but I couldn't find anything. It was like a shadow. I don't even remember the fire dingo. Wilbur told me he remembers it coming through. The creature seemed confused and it came over to us to check on what was happening. Wilbur tried to wake me and communicate with the clowder. He thought he got through but apparently not because no one knew what was going on."

Matt sighed and looked over at the cat. "Wilbur doesn't remember killing the fire dingo, but he must have because I was already out. The next thing I remember was Julia trying to wake me and we were curled up around the creature."

"Did Wilbur put up any protections?" Stuart asked.

"He remembers doing it but he wasn't sure how long they held. I'm not sure if they were up when Julia found us," Matt said. "I didn't think to check."

"You had no wards on you once you were in the house, but Wilbur was very weak so it's certainly possible they dropped during the night," Stuart said. Matt had only been moderately affected by the snow. Mostly his energy had been sapped and he'd slept. The fire dingo coming through was interesting. Almost as if Matt and Wilbur were meant to be saved.

Had Wilbur sensed something and used reflexive magic for protection and the fire dingo was what his magic called? If the dingo had had to go through multiple portals, that would explain the sense of confusion.

"That's all we remember," Matt said.

"It's enough," Stuart said. "I'll come back down with Amber and we can examine you again."

"Sure." Matt seemed unsure. Stuart left him, leaving the door partly open. The command cats probably knew about Wilbur's memories by now. They would have known as soon as Wilbur woke enough to convey them to Matt. The other clowder cats would have relayed the information.

Amber's room was on the second floor. Stuart had to pass by the library. Normally he liked the libraries, but this one was dark. Of course, the hurricane shutters were closed and there were few lights on. The brightest was in the back. No doubt Riley was at work back there.

Amber's door was open. She snored softly, her body spread out across her bed, visible even from the doorway. Minnett was next to her. Mack was also on the bed, his larger body curled around the little tuxie. Minnett and Mack stared at Stuart.

Moments later the soft snores stopped and Amber roused herself.

"Already?" Amber asked, her eyes barely open. Her skin looked pale. Stuart unfocused his eyes noting that her energy was still low.

"We need to examine Matt and Wilbur. Then Trag, Chase, and Courtney," he said. "Maybe even heal them if we can."

Amber nodded. She pushed herself off the bed without complaint. She paused to pull her hair back. Minnett leaped from the bed and followed. Mack was slower. Stuart wasn't certain but the cat may have glared at him.

DREW

Mack let Drew know that Amber and Stuart were up. Stuart was talking about checking on Matt first. Drew pushed himself away from the third floor window. The room was an unused one in the front corner of the house. A daybed rested beneath the window and Drew had been kneeling on it, watching out the window with Axel and Wheelie.

The snow came down hard enough now that he had trouble making out figures but it appeared that there were a couple of dozen people on the street. Two new cars had appeared and were parked in front of the house, one in front of the driveway, blocking them all in. That particular car looked sporty and red, which probably wasn't the best choice to try and block them in. Any good-sized truck could probably push it out of the way.

The people were moving, though the intelligence among them appeared minimal. Watching was boring, but Drew kept at it. The cats were more patient than he was. Now that Chase was settled, the window in his room covered, Drew had little to do. Until maybe now.

Everyone had watches, though some folks were napping so they'd be fresher for night duty. Too much coffee kept Drew awake and unable to rest.

He was frustrated with Chase. Chase had tried to let people into the house. If you couldn't trust everyone in the clowder, who could you trust? They couldn't even be sure Trag was safe any longer, not after what the cat had told them about Chase and breaking their bond.

Drew shuddered at the thought. He'd heard severing the bond was possible. He'd even talked about it with Mack but neither of them knew of specific stories or why it might be done.

"They're going down to see Trag first, instead of Matt," Mack said, referring to Stuart and Amber.

Drew sighed and left the daybed to head downstairs. They wouldn't need him for Trag. Unless something happened. Maybe if they needed to heal him, Drew could help hold the cat.

"I suppose," Mack said. *"It depends upon what they find. Minnett is with them, but she's still weak. Amber isn't completely rested either."*

Drew made his way down the stairs pausing at the second floor and then going down to the first floor. He heard Amber in the basement. He hurried a bit, not wanting to miss out.

Trag was up on one of the small round tables. Amber was in a chair. Stuart was standing. Both had their eyes closed, hands placed on Trag's side. Minnett wasn't touching Trag but sat on the back of the other club chair which was pulled up to the little table.

Drew waited by the stairs. He narrowed his eyes, hoping to see what they were doing, or perhaps get a sense of what was going on. Nothing. He was a guardian. He was strong and could fight, probably faster than anyone would believe, but he didn't see energies.

He looked towards Chase's door. The hairs on the back of his neck raised. Something was wrong in there. Drew walked over.

Elmore was crouched, his nose practically touching the wood. Kayley was in the chair. She looked up at him.

"You feel it too?" she asked.

"That sense that something's wrong in there?" Drew asked.

She nodded.

"Have you checked?"

"I was opening that door every five minutes for the first half an hour. I still check more often than I need to. He's on the bed," Kayley said. "I never see anything else. Elmore doesn't sense anything other than something is wrong. Like something is there and we can't see it."

"Could it be inside Chase?" Drew asked.

"Probably," she looked down, giving nothing away. No one wanted to think about what that might mean.

"Clear," Stuart said quietly. Both Kayley and Drew looked over. Amber was smiling.

Minnett jumped up on the table and sat with Trag for a moment, her body pressing against his.

"Trag has not been infected so far as any of them can see," Mack said quietly in his rumbling telepathic voice.

Drew walked over towards Stuart and Amber, but they were already leaving to go to Matt's room. He continued following. Minnett skipped past him as Amber got to the door. No one knocked.

"Time to be checked?" Matt asked.

Drew reached the door in time to see Amber and Stuart preparing to examine Wilbur. Drew stood by the door in case that triggered something in Matt. Minnett leaped on the bed. Wilbur still seemed out of it. Navy didn't much move, barely enough that they could touch Wilbur without feeling his presence.

Again, Drew saw nothing.

Matt was tense next to him, relaxing only when Amber nodded as she opened her eyes. She smiled at Matt. "He's clear."

Matt sagged slightly with relief.

"Your turn," Amber said.

The readings seemed to perk her up but her eyes still looked tired. Drew hoped she got through this and could rest before having to do more healing.

It took longer to scan Matt. Minnett hung back at first, before joining them, putting her white paw on his left thigh and looking up at him. The little cat flexed her paw slightly, like she was extending her claws, and then her eyes half-closed as she did her own examination.

Minnett finished about the same time as Amber. Drew felt his own muscles tensing up. They didn't need another Chase.

"Clear," Amber said. "Get some rest. Your energetic body looks worn out."

"Probably not nearly as bad as yours," Matt said.

"Probably not, but we need everyone as rested as they can be," Amber said.

Drew waited while Stuart and Amber passed. Amber gave his arm a squeeze. Drew took that as a sign that it was okay to follow.

They went to the medic room first. Drew hung back, not certain he wanted to go in there. Though it didn't feel as wrong as Chase's room, he sensed something. His whole body went on alert. The smell coming from the room was just a bit off.

"She used the restroom about half an hour ago," Mack said,

talking about Courtney. *"Julia and Cari thought to check on her."*

The smell was vaguely acidic but Drew wasn't thinking about a human smell. The scent eluded him and was gone.

Stuart and Amber stood next to the bed, blocking his view of Courtney. Minnett was on the counter behind her. Naturally, they wouldn't let her get too close unless Amber was there to protect the cat.

Drew walked over by the counter. If he had to rescue Minnett again, he wanted to be in place. Amber looked over at him and gave him a nod.

"She says thanks," Mack said. As if Drew needed a translation.

Minnett settled, ready to leap onto the massage table when they were ready. Stuart and Amber held hands and Amber closed her eyes. Stuart's eyes closed after.

They had barely started when the bed started to shake. Drew didn't see any reason for it. Courtney wasn't moving her body. If anything her muscles appeared too relaxed, like she'd gone to sleep. Drew tried to calm his heart rate. It was like a scene from an exorcism.

Minnett leaped over to the table. As she landed, Drew blew out a breath thinking he ought to have stopped her.

"She's needed," Mack said, his rumble bordering on a growl.

Drew moved closer. The bed continued shaking. From far away he heard the sounds of pounding on the hurricane shutters intensifying as if the people outside knew something was happening. The pounding came from all sides, louder than it should have been in the room. Drew looked over, blushing. He'd stupidly left the door open.

"Don't close it," Mack ordered. *"We think that it's better open."*

Amber started to slump forward, her head almost to Courtney's abdomen. Drew hadn't seen her do that before.

"You can hold her up. She's too weak for this. Courtney's fighting the examination and healing," Mack said.

Drew took a couple of steps until he stood behind Amber. He pulled her up, keeping his arms around her so that she didn't need to use her strength to remain upright. He felt her let her body sag down. He held her tighter, hoping he wasn't distracting.

Her hair smelled faintly of crisp clean soap. There was another scent there, too, the scent he associated with Amber, made up of the sweet smoky smell of moxa and fresh scented soap and a mixture of other things that were all her own.

Drew wished he could send her some of his energy. He hated that she was so weak.

A ripping sound reached Drew's ears as Courtney threw up her arms, both at once. The restrains had pulled loose from below. Courtney was pushing back at Amber and Stuart. She reached for Minnett who danced away.

Drew moved forward, placing a hand on Courtney's chest, using his strength to hold her down. It was awkward trying to hold Amber up with one arm and Courtney down with the other. He heard someone rushing down the stairs to help.

Julia rushed around the table and held a thrashing Courtney down. Tom came right behind her and went to the cabinet that held the restraints. Drew put both his arms back around Amber, keeping her from falling forward.

He focused on his own energy, of sending it out to Amber. Like a fisherman feeling a fish on a line, he felt Amber grab it and begin to suck it from him, drinking it in as fast as he let it flow.

"You need to stop," Mack warned.

Amber and Stuart appeared to be getting whatever was happening with Courtney under control. At least Courtney was no longer thrashing so much.

"Stop giving her your energy. You'll pass out or worse," Mack ordered.

Drew didn't know how to stop. Fortunately, at that moment, Stuart and Amber pushed themselves back from Courtney. Drew felt himself falling into a pile with the other two. He hoped they'd healed the young woman. He didn't have time to find out before his world went black.

The weird guy came back later, along with Amber. Courtney's heart started beating too quickly. This was it. Whatever they were going to do to her would happen now. No more waiting.

Her hands began to sweat.

Both Amber and the weird guy walked towards her bed, standing by the bed, looking down at her. Courtney closed her eyes, not wanting to see what they were looking at. She heard the door open again. This time it didn't close.

Amber placed a hand on Courtney's abdomen, her hand cold even with the fabric of the tank top to muffle the sensation. Another hand was placed there, equally cold.

Courtney's eyes sprang open but Amber and that man had theirs closed. They weren't even asking her anything. Not even going to talk to her like a human being. She was just a thing.

A thing with no power because they could do what they wanted. Heat started to rise up Courtney's back, the anger feeding it. It felt good to drown out the chill of the hands. Courtney closed her eyes, focusing on that heat.

Pressure increased on her belly. It was as if something was pressing a sharp point into her body and pushing through her skin and organs, digging in. The pain sharpened.

The pain fed the heat.

Courtney was certain she was going to die. If not from whatever Amber was doing then from the heat inside her. She felt the table starting to shake, the entire table. She wanted to hold on, but the pain was so great, she couldn't get her fingers to curl. If this was an earthquake, she needed to get out. They all needed to get out.

The pain grew.

Courtney's head started to throb and ache. Her eyes felt like they were on fire. Her mouth was once again parched and dry. Her lungs hurt.

The strength she felt was still building, using her pain and anger to create something new, something different.

Courtney pulled her arms up as hard as she could. She thought she heard something ripping, but the sound came from so far away. She struggled to push Amber off, to push the man away. She wanted to rip the restraints from her ankles, but hands forced her down.

She felt like someone was digging out her guts. Pain pushed up from her low back and then moved to her belly, like a giant spoon pulling out all her insides. Afraid to open her eyes, Courtney continued to struggle.

"*Let go,*" a voice whispered.

More hands touched her body, her chest, her abdomen, holding her down. She couldn't fight any longer. Courtney drew in a breath, feeling the ache as air hit her overheated respiratory system. Tears leaked at the edges of her eyes, drying quickly on the side of her face. It might have been her imagination, but she thought she heard a hiss of steam as her tears dried.

Courtney tried to let go, to relax her body. Her consciousness tried to hide in stories of her childhood.

When she was five years old, she'd gotten stuck in a closet. Her mom had been doing a huge spring cleaning. She'd pulled down everything from the big closet in the master bedroom and Courtney had gone in. Closing the door, something had fallen outside. Courtney couldn't get out.

She'd called and called, but her mom had gone downstairs. Terrified, Courtney had hugged her knees. A huge black and beige dog appeared beside her. In later years, Courtney couldn't say how it had gotten there, just that it had. The dog had snuggled its head against her chest. Petting it, her fears had disappeared at this wonder. They didn't have pets in their house. Her mom was allergic. The dog had been wonderful.

Relaxing, Courtney had been dozing when her mom came back upstairs. Vaguely, she'd heard her mom begin to move the boxes and continue sorting things, cleaning the stuff that needed to be cleaned, but Courtney said nothing. The giant dog had been lying next to her, his huge head on her lap.

Courtney liked the softness of his fur and the heat of his warm breath. She hoped that her mom wouldn't get rid of the dog. She'd fallen more deeply asleep at some point, safe in her mother's closet, surrounded by the comfort of the dog and the sounds of her mother.

An hour or so later, Courtney woke to the sound of her mom's puzzled laughter. Her mom had been confused as to why Courtney would decide to nap in the closet. The huge dog was gone. Her mom said it was a dream. Courtney was sure it wasn't.

Just like that, Courtney saw the black and beige dog in the room with her. Her eyes flew open to see him, sitting there, her one time savior, there to save her again. As an adult, Courtney noticed the broad, square muzzle and the hanging jowls. He was broader than a Great Dane but every bit as large. His eyes were deep chocolate pits, drawing her towards him.

Courtney tried to get to him, but she couldn't. The door was too far away, across the medic room, which was too bright on her eyes. She didn't know when the lights had come up.

The dog barked at her, baring his teeth. Apparently, he didn't want her to come to him.

Courtney huddled back against the table afraid to move. When she did that, the dog whined. Looking behind her, Courtney realized she was standing outside her body.

Her body wasn't still though. It was bucking and shaking and trying to throw off the people around her. There were four of them now. Amber's hand shimmered and pulled a thick, black, tarry muck from Courtney's belly. There were no wounds, no incisions. Just a shimmering hand pulling out blackness.

The dog whined again. Courtney turned towards it. She'd rather be with it. The dog growled at her.

Sighing, Courtney looked back down. She felt vulnerable without her body. It would be easier to stay where she was, but the room was getting cold. She'd been so hot and now she was cold. Suddenly. Weirdly.

She closed her eyes—did she have eyes? At any rate, she couldn't see. She thought about her body and then, *bam!*, she was back there. Too hot. Hands touching her.

Courtney pulled at her restraints. Her arms were free, though they were still buckled into restraints that were fastened to nothing. She pulled them off her wrists.

Fatigue leached through her and she laid back down on the table. The hands moved across her abdomen, touching her, examining her. It tickled. She almost giggled, but the effort to move her abdominal muscles hurt like she'd been doing hundreds of crunches.

Instead, she opened her eyes, this time for real. Stuart watched her, his eyes half-closed and unfocused. Courtney shuddered and turned away. As soon as he left, she'd take off the other restraints and make a run for it.

STUART

S tuart fell backward, feeling Courtney pull away from them. He'd been watching Amber pull out huge chunks of gunk from Courtney's body. He had helped Amber remove the gunk from her own hands. Minnett had worked more remotely than usual after Courtney started fighting, but Stuart had still seen the tuxedo cat's face looking over Amber's energetic shoulder.

The darkness in Courtney had looked like shadows or fog in her physical body. It had gotten darker in her energetic body, but still seemed amorphous. When Amber had tried grabbing it, it had become sticky, glopping onto her hands, stretching out from Courtney's body like melted cheese.

Stuart had felt himself tiring. Normally, even working that deeply shouldn't have depleted him so much. He'd looked around behind them and found snake-like creatures trying to fasten onto his energetic body, siphoning the energy. He used his magic to get rid of those, checking on Amber and Minett's energetic bodies. The snake-like things had ignored Minnett, but were going after Amber.

It was a moment's work to get rid of them.

Then, someone had begun feeding them energy. Amber worked faster after that.

Then, just as she was pulling the last of the tar goop from Courtney's energetic field, something had snapped and they'd all gone down.

Laying on the floor, Stuart examined himself. He was okay, if a bit more depleted than he should have been. No creatures appeared in his energetic field, or even his physical body. He examined the patterns of his energy and matched them against his known patterns. All good.

Then he sat up and looked over Minnett. She hadn't been in the pile, however, she had leaped off the counter and was nosing Amber. The cat's energy was okay. She hadn't been physically close to Courtney and nothing had grabbed onto her. Her patterns matched the patterns from before they had started the work.

Amber was pale and her breathing shallow. She had nothing attached to her now, but she was still worn out. Whatever had fed had taken the most from her directly. With Stuart helping strengthen her, she probably hadn't noticed how much energy was being stolen from her while she worked.

Still, she was in danger.

Drew was also on the floor, under Amber. He was breathing more deeply, but he looked as if he were worn out. Even his energy was dangerously depleted. Clearly, he'd been trying to help Amber continue her healing by offering her his own energy. Unfortunately, he didn't understand how to protect himself. His bond-mate must have been going crazy.

Tom pushed himself up on the other side of the table. He'd been holding Courtney down. "What happened?"

Julia sat up, looking equally dazed.

Stuart shrugged. He had ideas, but no certainties. He gave Tom a long look, checking his energetic body, but he appeared to be fine. Even his energy levels were better than anyone else in the room, except maybe Julia who was already standing and too far away for him to check.

Stuart pushed himself up and looked at Courtney. She looked back at him. Her eyes seemed clear. Unfortunately, he didn't know what her eyes looked like before. Stuart made a note of her energy patterns. Then he half-closed his eyes and examined her energy fields. Nothing appeared to him, but he wasn't able to look as closely as Amber would be.

When he opened his eyes, Courtney's were closed and she appeared to be sleeping.

"Watch her," Stuart said. He bent to help Amber up. She was sleepy but allowed herself to be led out of the room. Julia moved around to help him with Amber.

In the big room, that felt dark and boxy with the shutters closed, Stuart and Julia led Amber to one of the club chairs where she could sit. Trag was still on the table where he'd been examined.

He watched Stuart and Julia bringing Amber over with interest. Kayley noticed as well and she crossed the room to check on them.

"What happened?"

"Healing Courtney. I think we got it, but I'm not a healer so can't be certain. Can you have someone bring down food and maybe fruit juice? Soups would be good. Drew is also out," Stuart said.

Kayley nodded. She'd barely finished when Stuart heard people moving upstairs. The cats were no doubt relaying his orders to others.

"Tom is in the medic room. I'll need someone to stay down here and help him keep an eye on Courtney. I need to find a place to sleep. Amber might get up after some food. Send her and Minnett up for some sleep. I think eight hours would be a start."

Kayley's eyes were big and round, perhaps shocked that she was being pressed into service as a manager. Still, she was the one around.

Back in the medic room, Stuart and Tom put Drew on the massage table.

"After he gets some food, he should be able to leave. Even if he can only get to the club chairs, have him do it. I don't like leaving someone asleep with her, though it's safer now than it was. I'd rather minimize exposure until Amber examines her," Stuart said.

"Should I stay in here with him?" Tom asked.

"Definitely. Once he moves to another room, I'm thinking you can wait just outside the door. Julia's already out there. I don't trust whatever this is. Be mindful of Chase, too," Stuart said.

He hated that Chase was in the basement. But it couldn't be helped.

The stairs again looked formidable. Stuart pulled himself up, using the banister. He felt the wood, which was solidly affixed, shake slightly under his weight. He hoped he made it to the top. Each step was an effort, his feet feeling around to make sure they hit the next level, the height feeling impossible.

Finally, he dragged himself into the main room. Anson and Tenny were making food. Cooking, actually. Something was frying on the stove, something else heating in a saucepan. Tenny was pouring orange juice into glasses.

She looked up and saw him and brought one over.

"Thanks," Stuart said, letting himself sink down onto the sofa. His hand shook as he drank down the sweet juice. The sugars should help him perk up. Then he could make his own food or help out.

Until then, he laid back and fell into a light sleep, his mind running through healing patterns to hasten the speed at which he returned to his full abilities.

DREW

Hours later Drew woke up in his own bed. He remembered climbing off the massage table, which he had no memory of getting on and then going out to the main room in the basement. Someone gave him some orange juice, but he really just wanted coffee. Instead, he got soup and more food, which perked him up enough to go upstairs.

The house had felt strangely quiet and he was dozing off when Mack had said, *"No one is pounding on the hurricane shutters any longer."*

Maybe whatever Amber and Stuart had done to Courtney had gotten rid of the people outside. Drew rolled over and slept in a way he hadn't done in years. Maybe ever.

Vaguely he remembered dreams but they weren't bad dreams or weird dreams, just ordinary dreams of him doing ordinary things. When he finally woke, ready for a day, the house remained quiet. It seemed too dark. Of course with the shutters closed, it was dark everywhere, probably darker than normal with no lights from the street sneaking in.

Drew grabbed his phone to check the time. It was after ten at night. It had easily been six or seven hours.

"Six hours and forty-six minutes since you were in bed," Mack said. *"Amber is still sleeping, though Minnett said she is becoming more wakeful. Stuart is resting, though I am not at all certain he's sleeping."*

Mack was on the recliner that sat in the corner. Drew liked to read books there, mostly fantasy and science fiction, but sometimes he liked biographies. He liked figuring out what made people do useful things or how they fell into doing important things.

"What did I miss?" Drew asked. He talked out loud to the cat, keeping his voice down. Fin had the room next to him and if he was sleeping, Drew didn't want to wake him.

"Other than almost losing your life?" Mack asked.

"I did not almost lose my life," Drew said. "I feel fine."

"You were so depleted at the end, it would have been easy enough to do. A few more minutes and your body would not have had the energy to keep breathing. Kayley might have managed to save you because she was close, but with Amber out, you were in grave danger. While it was commendable that you thought you could help and may even have allowed Amber finish healing Courtney, I would ask that you not repeat the procedure."

Drew took the cat's admonishment to heart. He hadn't felt that he was that bad, but Mack saw things he didn't. The cats understood what could be done far better than he did. There weren't books, exactly, about how to work the magic that each of them got. It was all individual. Like all guardians, Drew had some extra strength. He was also good at anticipating the moves of an opponent. Tenny had gotten an increased patience for waiting out an opponent as well as greater balance.

In theory, these enhancements were based on the individual's genetics and abilities. However, all guardians tended to be stronger than a normal person of their height and weight. All healers had the ability to see into the energetic spectrum and work with it. How they worked with it was different from one to another.

Drew remembered that Bess was good at looking at someone and then telling them to do certain movements which she would mirror and the problem would be solved. Amber used her hands much more directly, like small needles. So did Minnett.

Maybe anyone could offer some energy but only certain people could protect their own.

"We all share energy," Mack said. *"You can be taught to protect your energy. Someone just needs to know how to do it. I could try and explain it to you, though I expect it would be easier coming from a human. Perhaps, later on, Minnett can talk to Amber and she can work out something that works for you. It is difficult for cats to determine what will work for a particular human."*

Drew changed clothes. The ones he had on felt ripe like he'd been sick. He went out to get food for Mack and to have a snack himself.

Stuart was stretched out on the sofa, apparently asleep. Julia was watching something on her tablet.

"How are things?" Drew asked, keeping his voice low. If Stuart were staying any amount of time, they ought to find him a room. The great room was where they gathered and talked and watched TV.

"Quiet. The people outside wandered off, a lot of them shivering and looking confused after Amber healed Courtney. A few stuck around longer, but they didn't seem as interested in getting in after that," Julia said.

Drew nodded, finding a frozen pizza and putting it in the oven. Not his favorite but it would do.

"The snow is slowing," Julia said. "Weather sites are saying the clouds are breaking up. It was moving north but the clouds just started disappearing, which is kind of weird the way it happened. I'm not a weatherman or anything, but it seemed like they thought it was odd, too."

"Maybe we got it out of Courtney," Drew said.

"Even if Courtney is clear, it's not gone," Stuart said from the sofa.

"How do you know?" Drew asked. He didn't like the guy. If he knew stuff like that, like how to get rid of this thing, he should have told them.

"Anything that comes through the portal must go back out. The portal hasn't opened since Courtney was cleared. Therefore nothing has gone back through," Stuart said.

Drew wanted to ask how Stuart knew that but watchers always knew. So did the cats. All the cats.

"*He's right,*" Mack said. "*Nothing has gone through. Whatever it is, it's not gone but it does appear wounded, or wants us to believe it is.*"

Drew frowned. Upstairs he heard someone moving around. Not long after, Amber appeared. She was still too pale, her hair lank. She seemed, somehow, diminished from her usual self. Minnett was with her, the cat following her, head tilted as if trying to keep watch on her bond-mate.

"Are we ready to work on Chase?" Stuart asked from where he laid on the sofa. He was still lying down and couldn't have seen her come down the stairs, not unless he had a mirror. Drew didn't know how Stuart knew it was Amber on the stairs.

Something else Stuart was keeping from them. Drew didn't like it. No matter what, he would make sure he stayed with Amber when she went into Chase's room to heal him. She needed someone watching her back.

"*Just don't add your energy to hers,*" Mack said. "*Your body can't take it.*"

Drew hoped that wouldn't be necessary.

STUART

Stuart was aware of Amber moving and waking in her room, though she was on the second floor and he was on the first. It wasn't a sound that reached him, just a knowing. The sense probably came from the close connection of having worked with her so often in the last few hours. Such knowing was not part of his usual talents. He was waiting for her when she appeared in the great room.

Julia made Amber eat. Drew hovered, glaring at him.

It was good for the clowder to be protective of each other, but sometimes people had to do what they were bonded to do. This was one of those cases. Amber needed to check Courtney and then work on Chase. Stuart intended to be sure she did that.

Just because the witches, or whatever they were, were less active at night did not mean they were weakened or gone. Many creatures were less active during the day or night, depending. Some were only active for a day once a week or month or some random amount of time that made sense in their world. Until proven otherwise, Stuart had to assume that this creature was as powerful as before.

Stuart followed Amber down the stairs after she had eaten something and chugged a can of Dr. Pepper, probably craving the sugar and caffeine.

The basement was dark and quiet. Fin was in a club chair playing cards with Matt. Matt looked more normal than he had earlier. Wilbur was curled up not far away, along with a petite Siamese girl. Probably Fin's Chara. Though small, she radiated power.

Both men nodded at Amber.

"Let's check Courtney first," Stuart said. Inside, Tom was gone but Tenny stood near the door, arms crossed. The way she looked over at them, unsurprised, Stuart knew her bond-mate Boyd was keeping her informed.

Amber went over to Courtney, who opened her eyes quickly before Amber even had a chance to touch her arm. She'd been waiting for them, too. Stuart thought that was interesting.

"How do you feel?" Amber asked the young woman.

"Like I want out of here," Courtney replied.

Stuart didn't blame her, but they needed to be sure she was clear first. He did a quick check on the energetic plane, but nothing appeared unusual or threatening.

Stuart grounded Amber as she went to check on Courtney herself. Minnett jumped up on the table. Stuart braced himself for something to happen, but other than Courtney shrinking away from the cat, it was fairly anti-climactic.

He watched Amber searching through Courtney's physical body. It looked a bit grayed out to Stuart, which wasn't normal but he couldn't put his finger on why. It could be fatigue. The poor young woman had just been inhabited by something powerful enough to utilize life force and cause hallucinations.

The energetic body looked clear. Again, it was faded as if

she were tired or worn out. Stuart thought he saw something move, something dark, but it was gone before he could focus on it. Then they were pulling out.

"Well?" Stuart asked.

"I think she's clear," Amber said. "Minnett isn't positive, but can't say definitively that she's not."

"What does that mean?" Courtney asked. She was still shrinking from the cat. Minnett apparently noticed and leaped onto the floor, her black tail waving in the air.

"I think that once we get you fed and the snow stops, you can go home," Amber said. "We have a guest room upstairs you can use. Third floor, but the bed is better than here."

"And you're not going to experiment on me?" Courtney asked, her voice small.

Stuart put a hand to his face, realizing how things must have looked. They were in a private medical room and the girl had been restrained for most of her stay. She'd barely been conscious of many things. No wonder she looked terrified.

"No," Stuart said. "You came to us with something inside you. I believe we managed to drive it out. Tenny can take you upstairs so you can rest."

"No cats will bother me?" Courtney asked.

It felt odd that she'd ask such a thing. Stuart realized that she'd dated Chase so she knew about the cats. If he'd understood correctly she and Chase had broken up in part because she didn't particularly like cats. It appeared that it was less a hatred and more a fear.

"They'll stay out," Amber said. "You'll have a private bathroom. The kitchen is a free-for-all but someone will help you find something you like."

Courtney's stomach growled in response making Amber smile. Stuart smiled, too. Courtney blushed just a bit but wasted no time getting off the table to go to her new room.

Stuart led the way out, preparing to go into Chase's room.

Elmore was still there, stretched out, his nose practically touching the door. The brown tabby moved as they got close, letting them by. He watched as Stuart and Amber opened the door.

Stuart's nose was assaulted by the smell of rot that hit him. The scent dissipated just as quickly as it had come. Amber stepped back and then stepped forward shaking her head.

Chase was stretched out on the bed, the covers thrown over him but not tucked in. One hand was over his head, the other on his abdomen.

"Chase?" Amber said quietly as they stepped into the room.

He mumbled something that Stuart didn't make out. They walked closer to the bed. Stuart turned to flip on a light and was startled to see Drew following them.

Reaching out to turn on the overhead he said, "You shouldn't be here. Your energy could get sucked into whatever is going on."

Drew stood his ground and crossed his arms. Stuart didn't have time to fight him or reassure him. If something happened to Drew, it would be on him, but at least Stuart could say, truthfully, that he'd tried to warn the guy.

Chase moaned a bit and then opened his eyes. The hand near his head went up to shade them.

"What?" he said.

"I need to do some healing," Amber said. The bed was low to the ground. Amber pulled the chair from the desk over and sat next to the bed. Chase watched her, looking nervous. Stuart filed that away.

He knelt next to Amber once she got comfortable. Minnett stayed on the floor but sat on Amber's feet. The cat started to purr, a soothing spell, probably for Chase.

Chase leaned back like he didn't care. He closed his eyes and his breathing turned deep and even almost immediately.

Something was off if the guy could fall asleep with the lights on and three people in his room. Stuart prepared to help Amber.

Going into Chase's body was very different from Courtney's. His organs were brighter but they cast shadows. Amber tried pulling those out. Stuart wished he'd remembered to bring jars.

He pulled out of the energetic healing and looked at Drew. "Get someone to bring in empty jars from the medic room," he said. Then he closed his eyes and went back in.

He noted Minnett looking over Amber's shoulder as Amber tried pulling out shadows. A jar was handed to her as she finished the low abdomen. She placed the shadows in there. They moved to the energetic level. It was hard to see anything, it was so filled with darkness.

Amber started pulling at it. While there was more darkness in Chase, it wasn't as thick and sticky as it had been in Courtney. Amber seemed to pull it, like a huge roll of cotton candy, forever. She filled several jars and even then Chase's energetic field seemed only slightly brighter.

Stuart had to give Amber credit. She continued on with her work. It was tedious watching her, but he didn't get tired as he had with Courtney. It was just scrapping the stuff out. Finally, the energetic field appeared clear.

Minnett pointed at something Stuart didn't see. Amber started to grab it. The film was nearly clear and started to wrap around her hand.

Minnett's energetic image pounced on it, like a cat on a bug, and grabbed the film off of Amber. They put the wiggling thing in a jar. Back at the physical level, a few shadows hid. Amber pulled them out.

When Chase looked as clear as possible, they slipped out of his body.

"I think that's it," Amber said. "Minnett wants to check him again tomorrow, though. Just in case."

"We'll need to take the jars back to the portal. To make sure whatever is in them goes back to where it came from," Stuart said.

Amber nodded. She stood up, rising easily. She seemed better than she had earlier. Maybe it was the caffeine. Stuart couldn't shake the feeling that after the challenge of working on Courtney, it should have been more difficult to work on Chase.

Minnett raced from the room as if she didn't want to stay there. Stuart frowned. The cat would have said something if there were problems. Yet, she didn't want to stay.

He wasn't sure what to think. At times he missed the connection of having a bond-mate to explain certain things to him.

The next morning, Chase ate a big breakfast. He missed the link to Trag but it would be up to the cat to reconnect them. He couldn't force it. Trag wasn't even in the same room as he was.

Chase practically licked the plate of eggs clean. Of course, everyone was eating well. Drew had a big breakfast and so did Amber. Amber looked pale and tired, worse, maybe, than she had when she'd walked into his room. Chase figured if she attacked him, he could take her.

An odd thought. He'd never considered fighting Amber. Riley plodded down the stairs and joined them in the kitchen. She just had coffee when she sat down.

"Stuart left to take the jars to the portal," Riley said.

Amber nodded. It was news to Chase. Of course, he didn't have a cat to let him know.

"Anson's with him," Drew said quietly. He seemed edgy as if he didn't trust Stuart.

"What do you think of that guy?" Chase asked.

"Stuart?" Amber asked.

Chase nodded. He looked longingly at her plate that still held half a piece of toast.

"He's okay," Amber said. "I mean, he's Base Command. We've always heard they were a little weird."

"I don't trust him," Drew said.

"He treated us well enough," Riley responded, sipping from her coffee. Riley would think that. She hadn't interacted with him, felt him take her power.

Another odd thought. It wasn't like Chase felt he had power. Trag had taken what little power he had when he'd severed the bond-mate link. Chase was weaker without the cat. He could feel it. Things he'd begun to take for granted like the ability to see better might not be gone but they weren't as strong. Of course, maybe it was just fatigue. He'd been out for some time. He'd even acted in ways that caused Trag to severe their bond. It would be normal for him to be tired.

"Minnett heard from Navy that the jars are through. Stuart set the portal to a lifeless world so they can't latch on to anything," Amber said.

"Will Anson return or is he on watch?" Chase asked. "I think today is my day, isn't it?"

"Normally," Amber said. "I don't want you on watch for at least a week, not until you feel better. Matt and Anson will work it out."

Of course, Chase realized he needed to be re-bonded with Trag. He was useless until then.

"Mostly Anson," Drew added. "Matt was out, too."

"I know," Amber said. "But his infection was different from Chase's."

Chase narrowed his eyes. He wanted to defend himself, that it wasn't his fault Trag had severed their bond. He wondered what he had done wrong to make it different.

Except he had no control over the infection if that was what she wanted to call it.

Courtney came down the stairs. She looked tired and washed out. Chase glared. He threw his silverware on his plate and left.

"Don't leave on my account," Courtney said.

"Not," Chase replied. He didn't know why he was acting like an idiot. The sight of Courtney made him itch. He rubbed his left arm, wondering what was going on.

Chase noted Amber watching him. He smiled at her and then turned and went downstairs. He didn't breathe out until he was back in his room. Safe.

He turned the light on. The board was still over the window. Chase got to work taking it down. He didn't like feeling as if he were in a prison.

Upstairs he felt Courtney sitting down to eat. Talking. Waiting.

COURTNEY

ourtney stayed the day at the clowder house, avoiding the cats. Amber checked her over several times while attempting to explain what had gone on. Apparently, the cats weren't normal cats. Or maybe the people in the clowder were all just crazy. Courtney couldn't decide. They were willing to let her go home later that evening, but Courtney chose to stay one more night. She wasn't ready to face her house in the dark. Alone.

Whatever had happened to her started there. Her house still felt like it was part of the problem. She liked the feeling of the clowder house, the way there were always people moving around. Even the cats bothered her less than the silence of her own home.

By the time she was ready to go, the snow had melted. She hadn't brought shoes coming over, so Cari found an old pair of tennis shoes.

Stuart and Julia brought her home. Stuart drove her over in his Range Rover. Julia drove Courtney's little Scion. The luxury of the Range Rover was amazing. Courtney hadn't realized a car could be so comfortable. For her, a car was a tool. After riding in Stuart's car, she decided she could get used to such luxuries.

Not that she could hope for nice things like that on her salary, though she did well enough for herself. Still, a woman could dream. Courtney ran her hands along the soft leather, the smooth dash. Everything was elegant and rich. It fit Stuart somehow, in the sense that he didn't feel like an ordinary person.

"Call us if you need anything," Julia said when they dropped her off. Both Julia and Stuart accompanied her into the house, Stuart walking through it as if he knew how scared Courtney was to stay alone.

"It's clear," he said. "No one here."

"Thanks," Courtney told them. Once they were gone, she went back to the bedroom to find her phone, still plugged in and charging. She had a call from Hannah and two from Payton. Plenty of texts from both of them and a couple from her mom and dad. She set about responding to them.

Faintly, she thought she smelled rot. Remembering her breakfast in the microwave. Courtney got up and sent it all down the garbage disposal. She didn't want to deal with the smell in her garbage.

Laundry took up time, the sounds of the washer and dryer familiar in the house. Her television worked. She talked on the phone to Hannah. Texted Payton. Let her know her phone hadn't been working right.

Tomorrow she'd go back to work. The streets were clear again, at least, though snow still huddled in the shadows beneath eaves and bushes. Life was going to go back to normal. Courtney couldn't wait to forget her encounter with a horror movie—make that several horror movies—and live her own life.

As she crawled back into her bed, her house whispered, "Courtney." Tears threatened. Amber had said things were okay. Maybe it was just her imagination. Courtney repeated the words to herself. Just her imagination.

Dozing off, she thought she heard the house laughing at her. Waking, eyes wide, Courtney looked around, her ears straining for odd sounds. The house remained silent. Courtney shuddered and pulled the covers closer to her, wondering if she was ever going to sleep again.

When the snows start again, Courtney must continue her battle with the creature inside her. Will she find the strength?

Check out the preview of *November Frost*.

Courtney knew she looked beyond haggard. The sleepless nights left bags beneath her eyes so large and dark that even if she dressed up in clown makeup they'd show through. She felt every bit of the fatigue that drew her lower lids halfway down to her chin.

Outside the billing office, she heard the sounds of patients and nurses talking, phones ringing, a dull white noise that didn't help keep her awake, particularly as the clinic was slow. People in Central Kentucky didn't like to drive in the snow.

It was barely mid-November and they'd had more snow than northern Canada. You'd think people would learn to handle the roads. The soft fire of the irritation woke Courtney enough to listen to Wendy, the assistant office manager, calling for attention.

"We're heading out," Wendy said. "All admin staff get to go home and expect to be off for several days. There's no break in the storm this time." Wendy sounded excited to be the one delivering the news. Courtney didn't care that much. What did she have to go home to?

The black office chair squeaked as Courtney stood. She bent to get her umbrella, something she'd taken to carrying. Her problems had started back in October when she'd gone out into the snow without covering her head. Some instinct suggested the lack of covering was the reason she was suffering now. Not from a cold or pneumonia, but from the terrors of a creature that called her name throughout the night and sometimes told her to kill people.

Courtney reached the coat closet first and grabbed her ski jacket. Usually, that was all she needed to stay warm. Lately, she'd been thinking she needed something warmer and when her brain was functional enough she took to pouring over LL Bean catalogs online.

It was something to do in the middle of the night when the house called her name.

Courtney had tried earplugs, which didn't work. She still heard her name being called. She tried using her earbuds and blocking out the sounds with music, but the voices interrupted the songs, singing her name at the most awkward times.

She'd gotten so desperate that one night, about a week ago, she'd called her friend Hannah to come over and spend the night. The voices were silent then. Nothing. No laughter. No written notes. Courtney felt rested for the first time in ages.

When Hannah left, and Courtney had put some clothes in the washer, her computer had started chanting, "Kill Hannah. Kill Hannah," in a robotic voice.

The worst part of the chant was that Courtney felt like she wanted to kill Hannah. She wanted to feel her friend's throat beneath her fingers, perhaps feel the silk of her hair as she ripped it from her head, watch as the light disappeared from her eyes. Courtney would drink in the warming terror of Hannah's last moments and be sated, at least for a few days.

The thoughts came from nowhere and everywhere. They made Courtney's stomach twist in knots and bile rise in her throat.

Her insanity, if that's what it was, began with the first snow and worsened every time the snow fell from the sky. One evening two weeks ago, before she'd invited Hannah over, the Christensen twins from up the street had been sliding around on the icy roads, pretending to skate. Courtney had been halfway down her driveway intending to break every bone in their bodies before she caught herself.

One day, she was going to wake with literal blood on her hands.

The first time it had snowed, she'd driven all the way to her ex-boyfriend's house to murder him. She hadn't remembered the drive. Still couldn't. Fortunately, he lived with people who seemed to understand what was going on.

The place was weird, the people weirder, but they and their magical cats had done their best to help Courtney. They thought they had.

But they'd failed.

Courtney kept intending to call them. Each time, her cell phone would go missing, or die, or the call wouldn't go through. Once she'd gotten her ex, Chase, and he'd laughed at her for trying to call.

Their house was across town. She could drive there today, instead of going home. Maybe they'd take care of her. They'd kept her from harming anyone last time. She might have hurt one of the cats, but it was just a cat, right?

Cats terrified her, but deep down, killing one would rip Courtney apart. She wasn't a killer. Yet this thing in her mind tried to make her into one.

Courtney waited by the side door of the clinic, stealing

herself for the cold blast that would come when she opened it. She wore heavy winter boots, solid ones that she had gotten from LL Bean, spending more money than she wanted on snow boots. Living in Lexington, you didn't really need such things. She'd been lucky. Hannah had tried to get some the next week but they'd been sold out. Too many people in Kentucky and Tennessee and Southern Ohio had been purchasing the heavy-duty boots in order to battle the unseasonably cold fall.

It was only November.

One of the other admins hurried over and paused before the door, both she and Courtney preparing as best they could to feel the cold that would eat away at their body heat more quickly than a school of piranha would finish a feast of two adults.

"You guys are lucky," Lori called over to them. Lori was a large woman with short hair who'd been a nurse at the clinic since before Courtney had started. Lori would be expected to continue working. She had a motherly attitude about her that made Courtney want to tell her all about the weird things that were going on with her.

Courtney had tried to talk to Lori once and she'd not been able to spit out a word. Finally, she'd ended up telling Lori that she looked particularly nice that day. A stupid thing. Lori had laughed. Courtney had laughed too and pushed it off on her fatigue. Even that opening hadn't allowed Courtney to say more.

That was one reason she hadn't gotten across town to Chase's. She needed to get there, one way or another.

That last thought warmed her as she thought about how nice it would be to squeeze the life of the people at Chase's, perhaps break some bones, wring the necks of the cats, or maybe kick one across the room. She dreamed of a sharp knife that would allow her to gut the weird guy, Stuart, who seemed somehow in charge even if he didn't live in the house. She wanted to know if his blood still ran red or if it had changed color.

The icy blast of air hit Courtney bringing her back to the present. She followed the admin through the door. She put up her umbrella under the awning wondering why she didn't think that Stuart's blood would be red.

ABOUT BONNIE ELIZABETH

Bonnie Elizabeth could never decide what to do, so she wrote stories about amazing things and sometimes she even finished them.

While rejection stung her so badly in person, she spent most of her young life talking to cats and dogs rather than people, she was unusually resilient when it came to rejections on her writing, racking up a good number of them.

Floating through a variety of jobs, including veterinary receptionist, cemetery administrator, and finally acupuncturist, she continued to write stories.

When the internet came along (yes she's old), she started blogging as her cat, because we all know cats don't notice rejection. Then she started publishing.

Bonnie writes in a variety of genres. Her popular Whisper series is contemporary fantasy and her Teenage Fairy Godmother series is written for teens. She has been published in a number of anthologies and is working on expanding her writing repertoire.

She lives with her husband (who talks less than she does) and her three cats, who always talk back.

Stay in Touch

ALSO BY BONNIE ELIZABETH

THE WHISPER NOVELS

Whisper Bound

Taken by the Sound

An Air of Suspicion

Little Dog Lost

Death Interrupted

Down in Whisper

A Haunting Whisper

A Haunting Attraction

Secrets Not Whispers

Only Human

APPALACHIAN SOULS

Souls Lost

Souls Broken

THE ASH JERICHO SERIES

An Inheritance to Die For

A Discovery to Die For

A Distraction to Die For

OTHER NOVELS

Ghosts from the Past

Unnatural Secrets

Find them all at your favorite bookseller or check us out at
MyBigFatOrangeCat.com